"Are you ready to meet your baby?" Elias asked.

"No," she answered, yet her hands were reaching out.

He watched as the baby's little almond-shaped eyes opened, and then the baby was delivered into his hands.

It was a little girl.

"Hey, baby," he said, and Beth watched as he smiled and saw that there were tears in his eyes. She was so glad that her baby had been delivered with love.

Somehow, at the scariest, most petrifying time in her life, she felt safe.

Dear Reader,

I had the opening to Elias's story in my mind for such a long time. Beth took a little longer to arrive, but the moment she did I was ready to start writing!

My gorgeous hero, Elias, is asleep during a lull in his shift in Accident and Emergency when he is woken and asked to come help with an emergency delivery. The trouble is, he knows the woman in labor; in fact, Beth is someone he has been unable to forget since their one night together, and judging by the dates…

We have all read stories about emergency personnel having to care for their loved ones, and I have seen it happen myself on occasion. It takes a real hero or heroine to push their own feelings aside and deal with such a situation, and I think Elias rises to the occasion very well.

I hope you enjoy reading Beth and Elias's story as much as I did writing it.

This is my 101st book. My 100th book, *The Innocent's Secret Baby*, is also out this month—if you enjoyed Beth and Elias's story, I hope you will enjoy *The Innocent's Secret Baby*, too!

Happy reading.

Carol x

THEIR SECRET
ROYAL BABY

CAROL MARINELLI

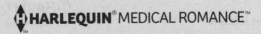
HARLEQUIN® MEDICAL ROMANCE™

Recycling programs for this product may not exist in your area.

ISBN-13: 978-0-373-21514-0

Their Secret Royal Baby

First North American Publication 2017

Copyright © 2017 by Carol Marinelli

Printed in U.S.A.

Books by Carol Marinelli

Harlequin Medical Romance

Desert Prince Docs

Seduced by the Sheikh Surgeon

The Hollywood Hills Clinic

Seduced by the Heart Surgeon

The Socialite's Secret
Playboy on Her Christmas List

Harlequin Presents

The Sheikh's Baby Scandal
The Innocent's Secret Baby

Visit the Author Profile page
at Harlequin.com for more titles.

CHAPTER ONE

'DID YOU GO home for Christmas, Elias?'

It was coming up for midnight and it was the first chance for the staff to have a catch-up after a busy few hours in Accident and Emergency.

Mandy, the nurse in charge tonight, had brought around a tray of coffee and cake and was in the mood for a chat.

'No.' Elias shook his head and took a very welcome drink as he wrote down his findings on Mr Evans—a patient that he had just referred to Cardiology.

'Did you work it, then?' Mandy asked.

Elias Santini was a locum Accident and Emergency registrar and, for the last few months, had worked at several locations across London, though he was fairly regular at The Royal. This meant that, as he became more familiar, people wanted to know more about his life.

'No,' Elias said. 'I just took a couple of weeks off and travelled. I saw in the New Year in Scotland.'

It was rare that Elias volunteered information about what he got up to in his personal life. Possibly he offered that sliver of information to distract Mandy from what he was sure she had been about to ask.

It didn't work, though.

The question still came. 'Where exactly is home?'

It would be easier to lie.

With his dark good looks and rich accent, Elias could say he was from Italy or Greece. He spoke both languages and could easily carry either off, but he didn't want to lie and neither did he want to deny his heritage.

He hadn't wanted to reveal it before.

Yet he was starting to feel ready to now.

'Medrindos,' Elias answered.

'Oh!' Mandy exclaimed. 'Mark and I went there on our honeymoon! We'd love to go back someday and see if it's still as beautiful as we remember.'

'It is,' Elias assured her.

'Where are you talking about?' Valerie, another nurse on tonight, asked as she selected a cake.

'Medrindos. Where Elias is from,' Mandy

told her. 'It's an island in the Mediterranean and it's stunning.'

It was, in fact, a small but extremely wealthy principality, though Mandy was right in her description. Medrindos really was stunning. It was an absolute jewel in the Mediterranean and an expensive holiday location. Mandy chatted about the pristine beaches and azure water, as well as the churches and the palace, while Elias carried on writing his notes.

And, while he didn't deny his country, he chose not to mention that he was a prince there, and second in line to the throne.

Soon, Elias knew from experience, he would be outed as a royal.

Maybe something would come on the news, or Mandy would go on the internet for a quick reminisce and would see pictures of the royal family, or she would read some headline about the errant young royals. His brother was currently kicking up his heels on board the royal yacht and partying hard in the South of France.

Elias knew he would soon be recognised, or the press would discover that he was working here, as had happened when he'd been a doctor in Oxford. The ensuing publicity had meant that the palace had summoned him home and for a couple of years Elias had lived the same depraved, albeit luxurious, lifestyle that his brother Andros adhered to.

Scandal had abounded but that didn't seem to matter, just so long as he remained in the fold. 'Princes will be princes,' his mother would say when another salacious article appeared. There had been one that hadn't been so readily dismissed. Elias had run into the inevitable trouble that awaited a man in his position—a heavily pregnant woman had gone to the press saying that she was carrying his child.

Despite Elias's assurances that there was no need for them to do so, the palace had set their lawyers and PR people into action. They had even worked out the payments should the baby prove to be his.

They had ignored two pertinent details, though.

Yes, there were pictures of the woman with Elias at a prominent London wedding and, yes, they had both attended the same gathering back in a luxury hotel.

But they hadn't slept together.

And had his mother known him at all, the other detail should have made her laugh at the absurdity of it all—the woman claimed Elias had told her he loved her.

Elias had never even thought, let alone uttered, those words to anyone.

No one had cared to hear that, though; instead, they had awaited the DNA result. Everyone, except Elias, had breathed a sigh of relief when the results had proved the baby was not his.

He had always known.

Elias had emerged from the *scandal* even more jaded—the life of a young single royal, though fun at first, had soon turned into what had felt a rather pointless existence. He didn't want to spend his life attending lavish parties, long-winded functions and openings, or getting wasted on the royal yacht.

It had felt empty and meaningless and when he'd discussed it with his parents they'd suggested that he marry. Princess Sophie of Theodora was their choice for him. They'd refused to accept his love for medicine and he'd refused to marry at his parents' command and so, six or so months ago, he had left it all behind and moved back to England, though to London this time.

He returned to Medrindos for formal occasions when his presence was required but here in London he relished the freedom of people not knowing his royal status. It came with its own unique difficulties—Elias held back from others and maintained his distance, yet it was a price that he had been willing to pay for this rare chance of normalcy and to do the job he loved.

Elias wanted more now, though.

He looked over as Roger, the consultant in charge tonight, returned from examining a patient.

'How's Mr Evans?' Roger asked.

'I've just referred him to Cardiology,' Elias said, 'but they're busy with a patient on ICU so it might be a while before they can come down and see him.'

'Why don't you go and grab some sleep while it's quiet?' Roger suggested.

Roger would finish at nine in the morning, whereas Elias was on call for the whole weekend.

It felt a little too early to be taking a break but he knew to seize the chance to rest when it arose, for it could be a long while before the department was quiet again.

'Sure.' Elias drained his mug of coffee but as he went to go, he changed his mind.

'Roger, I was wondering if I could speak to you on Monday.'

'You can speak to me now,' Roger said, but Mandy was hovering and Elias wanted to do this properly.

'I'd rather speak on Monday.'

'How about I come in at eight thirty?' Roger suggested. 'We can speak before you go home.

'I'd like that.' Elias said.

He walked through the department and around to the observation ward. Behind that was the staffroom and the on-call room.

An elderly gentleman who Elias had admitted to the observation ward a couple of hours earlier was singing 'I Belong to Glasgow', even though they were in the heart of London.

Elias shared a smile with the nurse sitting at the desk.

'I need earplugs,' she said. 'I think he'll be singing for a while.'

The singing followed him into the on-call room and Elias looked for the white-noise machine so that he could turn it on and block out the noise from outside.

He couldn't find it but knew that it would be in here somewhere.

Sometimes, if a new cleaner started, they put it away so he checked the cupboards.

There it was.

Elias turned it on and flicked off the light.

He kept his runners on and just stretched out on the bed and closed his eyes.

The white-noise machine was good but it

didn't completely block out the sound and he could hear the deep baritone voice.

'I belong...'

He was starting to feel that maybe he belonged here.

He liked London.

Oh, he would always belong to Medrindos, as his parents frequently pointed out. But he was starting to think that perhaps he could juggle both.

Yes, Mandy or someone else would soon work out who he was but he was prepared for that. He would soon turn thirty and knew he wanted to specialise in Accident and Emergency. He had completed two years of military service for his country but had then pushed to study medicine in England.

His royal status meant that it was impossible to practise medicine in Medrindos.

Elias loved his country very much and his parents ran it well.

And therein lay the problem.

It was a wealthy principality and there was very little for the second in line to the throne to actually do. His father, Bruno, was sixty and, with their genes, was likely to rule for another thirty years. His errant brother, Andros, would then take over the throne.

Elias wanted to pursue his career in medicine; he wanted to test and stretch his skills. He was thinking of applying for a placement so that he could become a registrar in the department and work his way up to consultant.

He drifted off to sleep. No dreams, no nightmares, no thoughts.

At least, not at first.

But then he fell into a deeper sleep.

Perhaps it was the strong Scottish accent from the vocalist outside that guided his dreams because his mind wandered back to that night.

The night he had walked away from it all...

There he was, aboard the royal yacht after weeks spent cruising around the Greek islands. On this night he and Andros were hosting a lavish party.

Princess Sophie was there, and not by chance.

It had been suggested by Alvera, Head of Palace Public Relations, that they be seen dancing tonight and that tomorrow they could be spotted on shore, having breakfast.

Their people wanted a wedding and to see one of the young Princes settled down.

He looked over at Sophie and she appeared as excited at the prospect of getting things started as he.

She gave him a pale smile.

Both their countries wanted this union and

were waiting with bated breath for it to start. Sophie and Elias knew that one dance, one kiss would mean that their *relationship* had begun. And even though it would all, for a while, be unofficial, to end things once they had begun would cause great embarrassment for Sophie and her family.

Better not to start things until they were sure.

And so, instead of walking towards her, Elias selected an unopened bottle of champagne and made a discreet exit.

No one noticed him leave and walk along the pier. He was dressed in black evening trousers and a fitted white shirt and was barefoot.

He walked onto the beach, enjoying the night and the feel of sand beneath his feet and the freedom. Not dancing with Sophie had bought him some time. Not much, as they were betrothed in their families' eyes. It really was just a matter of time before it was made official.

Oh, there would be a price to pay for refusing to toe the line but he was more than used to that.

Really, he only spoke with his mother when there was a scandal that needed to be ironed out or a tradition that needed to be upheld. It had been the same growing up. Queen Margarita had rarely put in an appearance in her sons' lives. There had been nannies to take care of all that. She might come into the nursery once the young Princes had been given supper to say goodnight.

His earliest memory was of his mother coming into the nursery. He had been so excited to see her that he had spilled his drink and she had recoiled.

'Can someone deal with Elias?' she had asked.

They had moved on from spilt milk but the sentiment was the same.

Elias, though, neither wanted nor needed to be dealt with.

His and Andros's job was to stand by her side during public appearances.

Elias wanted more.

He didn't want to marry and he was tired of partying and meaningless sex. He turned and looked out towards the yacht. The laughter drifted across the water and he was simply relieved to be away from it.

Yes, his mother would not be pleased that nothing had happened between him and Sophie but Elias refused to be compliant.

He was bored, he realised. He missed being part of a team and using his brain. His father had suggested an advisory role on the board of Medrindos Hospital and Elias could think of nothing worse.

He uncorked the champagne and it was then that he heard a voice.

'Celebrating?'

He turned and saw that he did not have the beach to himself—there was a woman sitting beneath a tree with her legs stretched out and her hands behind her as if she was sunbathing beneath the moon.

'I guess I am,' Elias said, though he didn't add that the champagne corks popped at lunchtime every day in his world.

'And I thought this was *my* slice of heaven.'

'I didn't mean to interrupt,' he said, smiling at her soft Scottish accent.

'It's fine.'

He saw that she had a plastic glass in one hand and he held up the bottle, offering her a drink of champagne. He saw her teeth as now she smiled.

'I thought you'd never ask.'

He walked over and filled her glass and he could see that she had long curly hair but he could not make out the colour.

'Cheers!' she said.

'Cheers.'

They both took a drink, she from her plastic glass and he from the bottle, and it was pleasant.

'They sound as if they're having fun,' she said, and nodded in the direction of the yacht.

He didn't tell her that that was where he had just come from, or that he hadn't been having fun in the least.

'They do. I'm Elias,' he introduced himself, but then frowned as he did so—*Elias* had been said in a woman's voice that wasn't his.

'Elias!'

His eyes snapped open as he realised that it was Mandy who had just invaded the memory of that night. He sat up straight as the door to the on-call room opened and the bright light from outside hit him and that long-ago night was left behind.

Immediately his feet were on the ground. He knew, from the sharp knock at the door and the call of his name, and from the fact that Mandy had come directly to get him, that it was serious.

The reason she hadn't simply called him to come around was because she had been busy making another urgent call on her way.

As they walked swiftly through the department she brought him up to speed.

'I've got a young woman in premature labour. I've just put out an urgent call for the obstetric team but it's bedlam in Maternity apparently.'

It happened at times.

The obstetric team wasn't sitting around, drinking coffee and waiting for an urgent call from Accident and Emergency. Last month Elias had delivered a baby boy before they had arrived.

That had been an easy delivery, though, and the baby had been full term.

This one wasn't.

Chimes started to ring out as Mandy explained further. 'Mr Evans has deteriorated, I've put out an arrest call and Roger is in Resus with a sick child.'

The department had, as it so often did, just got extremely busy.

'How pregnant is she?' Elias asked.

'Twenty-nine weeks. Her waters broke as we got her onto the gurney. Elias, this baby is coming and very rapidly.'

They had reached the cubicle and Elias took a steadying breath. He hadn't dealt with a premature baby on his own before.

He heard a low moan of pain from behind the curtain.

'What's her name?'

Before Mandy could tell Elias he was already stepping into the cubicle.

And before Mandy said the name, he knew it. 'Beth.'

She was sitting up, wearing a hospital gown, and there was a blanket over her. Her stunning red hair was worn up tonight but it was starting to uncoil and was dark with sweat. Her gorgeous almond-shaped eyes were for now screwed closed and she wore drop earrings in rose gold and the stones were rubies.

They were the same earrings she had worn the night they had met.

He could vividly remember stepping into her villa and turning the light on and watching the woman he had seen only in moonlight come into delicious colour—the deep red of her hair, the pale pink of her lips and eyes that were a pure ocean blue.

Now Valerie had her arm around Beth's shoulders and was telling her to try not to push.

For Elias there was a moment of uncertainty.

Could Mandy find someone else perhaps? Could he swap with Roger?

Almost immediately he realised there was no choice. Being brought up to speed on Roger's ill child, and having Roger brought up to speed on Beth, would lose vital minutes for both patients.

They were already stretched to the limit.

And from what Mandy had told him this baby was close to being born.

His baby?

He could not afford to think like that.

'Beth,' Valerie said. 'Dr Santini is here…'

Yet her eyes had already opened and met his and recall was instant for she would remember that night for ever.

Not just the romance and kissing and not just the delicious love they had made.

But that the results of that night had torn her life and her family apart.

CHAPTER TWO

BETH FRANTICALLY SHOOK her head when she opened her eyes and saw that Elias was there but then she saw he was wearing navy scrubs.

Squinting, she read his name badge and it registered that he was the doctor who had been summoned to treat her.

She simply didn't have the breath to speak yet, but she did not want to see him like this, or for him to find out he was about to become a father like this!

Everything was going wrong.

Rapidly so.

Fifteen minutes ago she had been patting herself on the back for a job well done and about to cross the street from the restaurant she had just left and head for the hotel. Now she stared into the eyes of her one and only one-night stand.

Elias.

All Beth wanted was to go back to the hotel

and to wake up in the bed there and declare this a bad dream so she tried to climb from the gurney.

'I want to go home.'

'Beth, you need to lie back,' Valerie said, and held her, but Beth shrugged off the arm and as she did so she lost the gown.

'I can't...' Beth said, and she rattled at the side of the gurney. 'I want to go back to the hotel. I want...'

Elias caught her hands. He recognised her anguish and knew enough to be sure that it was not simply down to his presence.

She was in a rapid, tumultuous labour and that was a very scary place to be.

'You're okay.'

His was the voice of reason and she wondered if he even recognised her, he was so completely calm when everything, *everything*, was going wrong.

As an events co-ordinator, Beth was here in London for the opening of Mr Costas's London branch of his renowned restaurant.

He was her top client.

The night had gone beautifully and to plan. The restaurant had been filled mainly with friends and relations of Mr and Mrs Costas. Most had travelled to London for the occasion and, because she had liaised with a lot of the guests for a previous event, the opening night had been easy to organise. The hotel opposite the restaurant was hosting the guests and all had gone well.

It had only been at the very end of the night, as the last of the guests had left, that Beth had suddenly felt terribly warm.

She had been wearing a black light wool dress, sheer black tights and high heels and, despite it being a cold night in early January, she hadn't put on her coat.

The cold air had been welcome on her burning cheeks and she had taken a moment to gulp it in. She had just started to walk when she'd felt a sharp pain in her back.

It was the high heels, Beth had decided, but the pain had been acute enough to stop her and, even though the pavement was wet, she had bent to take her shoes off.

The pain, though, as she'd bent over, had stretched from her back and wrapped around her stomach like a vice, and Beth had placed a hand over her bump and felt that it was hard and tight.

As the pain had passed she'd straightened up and leant against a wall, trying to get back her breath.

She'd been standing in stockinged feet, holding her shoes, when she had broken out into a cold sweat and suddenly felt as if she might vomit.

The hotel, even though it was just across the street, had seemed a very, very long way off.

It had happened as rapidly as that.

Beth had taken out her phone and stared at it, wondering who she should call, trying to fathom what to do. Should she call the hospital she was booked into?

But that was in Edinburgh.

Did she need an ambulance?

No, she decided.

The pain had gone now.

Was it perhaps the beginnings of an upset stomach?

She tried to console herself that it was that.

Even if it meant that all Mr Costas's family and friends were bent over a toilet right now, somehow she convinced herself that she must have eaten something that had disagreed with her.

But then another pain came.

It wasn't as severe as the first but it was way more than the practice contractions that the midwife at her last antenatal visit had told her to expect. Then she felt a pulling sensation low in her pelvis that had her gasp and it felt as if the baby had shifted lower and was pressing down.

She knew she had to get to hospital and she saw a taxi and stepped forward and hailed it. Thankfully he slowed down.

'Can you take me to the nearest hospital?' she asked.

'The Royal?'

'Please.'

Beth sat there with her heart hammering, telling herself she was overreacting and wondering who she could call.

Her parents?

Immediately she pushed that thought aside.

They were furious and deeply embarrassed that she was pregnant and wanted nothing to do with her for now.

Oh, her mother visited occasionally and came armed with knitted cardigans and booties, and her father had sent her a card with a long letter as well as a cheque to buy some essentials for the baby.

It wasn't the child's fault, he had said in his letter.

She thought of calling Rory, her ex.

Only it wasn't fair to call him after midnight when there was nothing he could do.

It wasn't as if it was his baby.

Beth willed herself to stay calm.

The pain had stopped and even if she was in labour she knew that there were drugs that could be given to halt it. That had happened to a friend of hers. Yes, she'd be stuck in London perhaps for a little while but she could handle that.

Just as long as the baby was okay.

Then another pain hit.

And this was even worse than the first had been.

So much so that Beth let out a long moan as she fought the urge to crouch down on the taxi floor.

'It's okay, love,' the taxi driver called out. 'We're just about here.'

He stopped the taxi outside the Accident and Emergency department and started sounding his horn and making urgent hand gestures for someone to come and assist. Beth watched as a security guard raced inside.

The pain had passed but it felt as if her legs had turned to jelly and she couldn't move. She was starting to shake yet she was still desperately trying to cling to the denial that her baby was on the way. First babies took for ever, Beth knew that, and she had only had a few contractions. She was fine, so much so that she went in her purse to pay the fare.

'How much is it?' Beth asked in a voice that sounded vaguely normal.

'It's okay, love,' the driver said. 'This one's on me.'

'Here,' Beth said, and held out some money, but he didn't take it. *'Here!'* she shouted when she never, ever shouted.

She wanted this to be a normal taxi ride, not an emergency one.

'You'll take my money!' she told him.

It was imperative to stay in control—Beth had been taught to.

There might be a wild, feisty streak that ran through her but she had long ago learnt to suppress it.

Bar once.

That lapse was the reason she was here to-night.

Beth didn't want the sight of two nurses coming towards her and pushing a wheelchair. She handed over the money and watched as the door was opened by one of them.

'I can make my own way,' she said, yet her hand was now gripping the handle above the window and she was again fighting not to bear down.

'Let's help you out,' a nurse said.

With no choice, Beth accepted the waiting hands that helped her out.

She was still carrying her coat and shoes yet she was shaking all over.

'I'm Mandy,' a nurse told her, 'and this is Valerie. What's your name?'

'Beth.'

'How far along are you, Beth?' Mandy asked as they helped her into a wheelchair.

'Twenty-nine weeks.'

They pushed the chair into the department and Beth could see that it was busy.

The doors to an area opened and she glimpsed a lot of staff around what looked like a very sick child and a man receiving cardiac massage.

Shouldn't these nurses be in there, helping?

Yet they were both still with her and had wheeled her into a cubicle and were helping her to stand and asking questions about the pregnancy and how long she'd had pain for when she felt a warm gush between her legs.

'I've wet myself…' Beth whimpered, and she started to cry with the indignity of it all as they helped her up onto the trolley.

Mandy was peeling off her underwear and tights and Valerie was trying to get her out of her dress as a receptionist came in.

Why was a receptionist here when she was nearly naked? Beth wanted to ask. She was a very private person and it felt appalling to be exposed but then Mandy covered her with a blanket.

Beth saw Mandy's worried look as she took a phone out of the pocket of her uniform and suddenly she had gone.

'We need your full name and address,' the receptionist said.

They didn't seem very relevant to Beth right now.

'Elizabeth Foster.'

'And I need your address, Elizabeth.'

'Beth,' she loudly corrected, and realised she was shouting again but she hated being called Elizabeth—that was the name her parents used when they were cross.

Oh, and they'd been cross of late.

'We need your address…'

Beth gave it.

'You're a long way from home,' Valerie commented.

'I'm in London tonight for work.'

'We need a next of kin.' The receptionist was still asking questions but Beth was finding it hard to focus let alone answer and she shook her head. She did not want them contacting her parents about the baby when they had been so angry and had said they wanted nothing to do with it but then Valerie spoke gently.

'If something happens to you, Beth, we need to know who to call.'

And though she was currently upset with

her parents she thought of them in the middle of the night being called with bad news and she didn't want that for them.

'Rory...' Beth gasped.

He would know how to handle them.

'Is that your partner?' the receptionist checked.

'No, he's my ex but he's a very good family friend, he knows all that's happened, he'd know how best to tell my parents if something happened to me.'

'What's his phone number?'

'It's on my phone.'

She found the number and then watched in terror as a resuscitation cot was brought into the cubicle and plugged in.

'It's too soon,' Beth pleaded. 'Can't you give me something to stop it?'

Surely they were going to stop the labour—she was only twenty-nine weeks.

'It's okay.' Valerie put an arm around her.

'I need to push.'

'Don't push,' the nurse said. 'Wait till the doctor's here.'

Beth screwed her eyes closed and fought not to push. It was like trying to hold back the tide yet she did all she could to hold her baby in.

Everything was going wrong.

Every last thing.

Because she opened her eyes and suddenly there he was.

Elias.

Her one-night stand, the father of her child.

'No.'

She actually tried to launch herself and get off the trolley and declared she was going home.

She simply wanted to run.

Yet there was nowhere to go, the logical part of her brain knew that, and so did he for he caught her hands and held her loosely by the wrists as she knelt up on the trolley with the hastily put-on gown falling over her shoulders, and she knew her breasts were exposed.

And she cared not a jot any more.

He was so calm that she actually thought he might not recognise her.

Beth knew she would never forget him.

She had never thought she would see Elias again and yet she was staring into those grey eyes that had so easily seduced her and it was all too much to take in.

He was wearing rumpled navy scrubs and his hair was longer than it had been when they'd met. Now it fell forward and she wanted to push it back from his eyes, and she saw that unlike when they had met he was unshaven.

He looked as if he had just woken up.

'Beth,' he said. 'The obstetrics team is on the way. For now, though, it's me.'

She just stared back.

'I'm one of the doctors working in Emergency tonight and I need to examine you.'

There was no choice, Elias knew.

He was the only doctor available in a critical situation.

Not that Beth understood.

'Oh, no!' She shouted it out. 'I want an obstetrician!'

Valerie squeezed her shoulder.

'Dr Santini knows what he's doing,' she reassured Beth. 'He's an emergency registrar. Just last month he delivered a lovely baby boy. You're in good hands, Beth.'

It wasn't his bloody qualifications she was objecting to.

It was the man himself, the man who, as Valerie helped her lie back, was calmly putting on a paper gown and then had the nerve to put on gloves.

'You stop to…?' She didn't finish but Elias got the inference.

He had intimately explored her with his fingers, why worry with gloves now? And, no, he hadn't stopped to put on a condom.

Here, perhaps, was the consequence.

He couldn't think like that now. He could

not addle his mind with the thought that he might be about to deliver his own child.

'We need to focus on the baby,' he said, and Beth looked at him and saw that despite the very calm demeanour there was concern in his eyes.

Serious concern.

'Can she have some oxygen on?' he asked Valerie, who was trying to pick up the baby's heart rate with a Doppler machine.

The gown had long since gone.

She was naked, scared and vulnerable.

'Can I examine you, Beth?' Elias checked.

She could hear the chimes going off again. They were calling for an anaesthetist now and she thought of the man being given CPR. She had heard the nurses discussing the very sick child and if more staff needed to be sent down.

It was down to Elias, she realised.

Maybe this was hard for him too, she thought, because now she knew that he recognised her, for his voice was a touch strained as he requested her consent.

She nodded and then she told him her fear and why she was so confused.

'It's happening so fast. Just *so-o-o* fast. I was fine.'

'How long have you been having contractions for?' Elias asked, as Mandy helped her to lie down and lift her legs.

'I don't know,' Beth said, and then she remembered standing outside the restaurant and looking at her phone as she pondered what to do.

'Midnight.'

Elias glanced up at the clock—it wasn't even twenty past twelve.

Poor thing, Elias thought.

Not just because it was Beth.

It was called a precipitate labour, one where the uterus rapidly expelled the foetus, and, though premature babies often came faster than full term ones, this was very rapid indeed. The contractions were often violent and exhausting, and the mother presented as drained and shocked.

'Can you give me something to stop the labour?' Beth asked as he examined her, and then she saw Elias's jaw grit.

'Beth, your baby's about to be born. There's nothing I can give you to stop it. We want to slow this last part down as best we can. You're not to push...'

He would try and control the delivery with his hand as a very rapid birth could damage the baby's brain, and also he badly wanted assistance to be here when the baby was born.

He looked over to Mandy.

'Should we move over to Resus?' he asked quietly, because there were more drugs and equipment over there, but Mandy shook her head.

'It's full. We've got everything in here and the team are on their way.'

Elias nodded.

He had seen them at work several times. They came with everything that was required. They could turn this room into a neonatal intensive care ward and also a theatre, if such was needed for Beth.

He was very glad to know that they were on their way.

His fingers were on the baby's head, trying to control the delivery, and, unlike the large baby he had recently delivered, this head was tiny to his hand. 'It's coming again,' Beth said. 'I have to push,'

'No, no,' he told her, but not dismissively, more he suggested that she could resist. 'Breathe through it, Beth. Take some nice slow breaths.'

She was taking short, rapid ones.

'Slow breaths,' he reminded her. 'Let's try to give this little one a gentle entrance to the world.'

Another contraction was coming and she

moaned through the pain and the agony of not pushing when every cell in her body demanded that she do just that.

'It's too soon,' she sobbed. 'The baby's too early...'

'It is what it is,' Elias said as the pain passed.

Odd, but those words calmed her.

They were the words her father used when one of his parishioners came to him during a tumultuous time in their life. Always Donald was calm and wise. He would listen as they poured out their dramas and fears, and then those were the words he would recite—*it is what it is*—and then he would do what he could to help them move forward.

Her father, though, had not been able to do that with her. It had been too much for Donald to accept that his gorgeous, well-behaved daughter had run so wild, let alone offer guidance.

Now Elias did.

His voice was assertive as he told Beth what to do and she was ready to listen.

'Keep taking some nice deep, slow breaths so that your baby gets plenty of oxygen.'

She could do that.

'Focus,' Elias said.

'I'm trying to but—'

'Nothing else matters now.'

It didn't.

His words were for both of them, a secret conversation between them, and he glanced up as he said it. 'Just focus on the baby, the rest can all wait.'

Their history was irrelevant right now.

He could see that the baby was a redhead like its mum, but he would let Beth find that out for herself.

Any moment now.

He looked over at the equipment that was all set up and at the cot that was now ready and waiting. The overhead lights would warm the little one and he gave Mandy a small nod of thanks because she had it all under control. She was pulling up a drug that would be given once the baby was born to help with the delivery of the placenta.

There were scissors and cord clamps waiting. There was a sterile wrap she would take the baby from Elias with. And there was a little moment of calm.

'You're doing so well, Beth,' he said.

He meant it.

She was exhausted, her auburn hair was as wet as if she'd just come from the shower. Her already pale skin was bleached white so that her freckles stood out.

And yet she was calm now.

Resigned that her baby was coming, whether she was ready or not, Beth was doing all she could to take slow breaths so that more oxygen could get to her child.

Valerie had found the baby's heart rate with the Doppler and it was strong and fast and it felt as if it was the only sound in the room.

'Do you know what you're having?' Valerie asked, and Beth shook her head.

'I wanted it to be a surprise.'

And, at the oddest of moments, she and Elias shared a small smile.

It was certainly that.

Then she stopped smiling.

'Another one's coming,' Beth said.

He heard her hum, and then she hummed louder and her thighs were shaking as she fought not to push.

And though Beth didn't push, her uterus contracted and the head was out.

The cord was around the neck but only loosely and Elias slipped it over the little head.

'Are you ready to meet your baby?' Elias asked.

'No,' she answered, yet her hands were reaching out.

He watched as the baby's little almond-shaped eyes opened and then the baby was delivered into his hands.

It was a little girl.

'Hey, baby,' he said, and Beth watched as he smiled and saw that there were tears in his eyes. She was so glad that her baby had been delivered with love.

Somehow, at the scariest, most petrifying time in her life, she felt safe.

He held the baby as Mandy clamped and cut the cord. She was blinking at the world and taking her first breath, startled. Her eyes screwed closed and then her mouth opened and she let out a small, shrill cry. As Mandy went to get the sterile sheet to take the baby from him, instead Elias passed her to Beth's waiting hands.

That moment of contact with the baby had felt such a vital one that he wanted Beth to experience it as well, as he knew it would be a while before she got to hold her again.

The baby was vigorous and had started to cry as she was born but calmed as she met her mother.

'A girl,' Beth said, as her baby was passed to her, and she scooped her in.

The baby lay stunned on Beth's chest like a shocked little bird recovering from a fright. The little eyes were open as she breathed in the scent of her mother and listened to the familiar sound of her heart.

Mandy put a blanket over the two of them and held oxygen near the baby's face as Elias came over to do the initial assessment of the infant.

He could not afford to think of her as his so he pushed that aside as he checked the baby.

Her heart rate was rapid and her breathing was too and she was pink.

It was a moment.

Less than a moment that mother and baby shared.

Yet it was such a precious time. There was a beautiful time of calm and peace as she met her little girl.

'Oh, baby,' Beth sobbed, and she held her little daughter to her naked skin.

All the problems that had got her to this point just disappeared as she gazed at her baby and met her eyes.

'We need to get her over to the cot,' Elias said.

'Let me hold her a little while longer.'

'Beth, I need to check her.'

He could hear footsteps running towards them as he peeled back the blanket and lifted the baby off Beth. The baby cried in protest at the intrusion as he took her to the warmed cot.

'How is she?' Beth was calling out.

Her one-minute Apgar score was a seven,

which, given how premature she was, was good. Her muscle tone was low but that was to be expected with a gestational age of twenty-nine weeks.

Elias handed over to the obstetrics team and watched as they set up their own equipment.

Mandy had dashed off again.

It was becoming increasingly noisy outside the cubicle but Elias couldn't think about what was going on out there now.

He stared down at the little baby and with every passing minute she became increasingly exhausted, unlike the vigorous baby that had been delivered.

He could see that her nostrils were now flaring, which was a sign that she was having trouble getting enough oxygen, and her limbs were flaccid.

'Elias…' Mandy put her head around the curtain. 'I need you.'

'In a moment,' Elias said.

'I have a two-year-old convulsing…'

He just stared at the baby.

'Elias,' Mandy called loudly, on her way to Resus.

He looked over at Beth, who was being comforted by Valerie. A midwife was looking after her too but for a brief moment she glanced at him.

'Elias!'

His name was called again and an emergency bell sounded and there was nothing he could do for his baby.

Even if he told them that she was his, he would just be asked to step aside.

And so he did what, as a doctor on duty, he had to do.

'I'll be back…' he said to Beth, but she wasn't looking at him now. She was in the third stage of labour and about to deliver the placenta while looking over anxiously at the crowd of experts around her baby.

His.

He allowed himself to acknowledge it then. The baby was his.

CHAPTER THREE

ELIAS HAD GONE.

She could hear him being urgently summoned and understood that he had no choice but to leave.

Actually, no, Beth didn't understand anything.

It was twelve twenty-nine and less than half an hour ago she had been standing in the street, wondering what to do.

Now she was a mother and no one could tell her how her baby was.

She heard the odd word.

'Surfactant.'

'Struggling.'

'Grunting.'

'CPAP.'

'I want her on the Unit,' someone said.

Beth lay back, shivering under a blanket, as a midwife checked her blood pressure and listened to what was being said.

'There are no cots. She'll have to go to St Patrick's.'

There were voices with no names and she felt dizzy as it dawned on her they were talking about transferring her baby.

'You're not taking her to another hospital.' She shook her head. 'No.'

'It's okay,' the midwife said. 'We'll get you over there as soon as we can.'

'I want to be with her.'

An IV had been inserted and Beth couldn't even remember it going in.

'Her blood pressure is ninety over fifty,' the midwife called, then spoke to Beth. 'What's your normal blood pressure?'

She couldn't answer.

Beth tried to explain that she'd been told at her checks that her blood pressure was on the low side but she couldn't remember the numbers and there were little dots swimming before her eyes. Her lips had gone numb.

'I'm just going to lay you flat,' the midwife said, and Beth felt her head drop back. 'Take some deep breaths.'

Again.

The only noise she could hear was the heart monitor on her baby and it sounded fast, though she wasn't crying now and hadn't been for a while.

Beth lay there trembling at the shock and the speed of it all.

A man who said he was a neonatologist came and told her that her baby was about to be transferred and that NICU was the best place for her now.

'Can I go with her?'

'No.' He shook his head. 'We've got a lot of equipment and staff that will be travelling with her.'

'I'll not get in the way. I'll just sit.'

He didn't wait to explain further that she was in no fit state to sit.

'Can I see her?' Beth asked, but her baby was already being moved out and all she got was a tiny glimpse of red hair and the sight of tubes and machines and then she was gone.

It was very quiet in the cubicle after she left.

Mandy came in with another flask of IV fluid and it was checked with the midwife. 'I've ordered an ambulance for you, Beth. It might be a while, though, they have to deal with emergencies first.'

Thankfully it was only fifteen minutes or so before she was being moved onto a stretcher.

The midwife would escort her and all that was left to do was thank Mandy, who gave her a smile.

'I'll ring before I leave in the morning and

find out how your baby is doing. Do you have a name for her?'

'Not yet,' Beth said.

She'd had a couple in mind. Eloise was one, because it was close to her baby's father's name.

Beth could see Elias working away in Resus as she was wheeled past.

She was taken out into the night and loaded into an ambulance where she could hear the controller speaking over the radio.

It was a ten-minute ride through dark streets and soon she was being taken through corridors and then in an elevator up to the maternity ward. As she was wheeled along a corridor she could see signs for the NICU further along and knew her baby was there.

'How is she doing?' Beth asked as she was moved onto a bed.

'As soon as we hear anything, we'll come and let you know.'

She was told that over and over again.

Beth had never felt more scared and helpless in her life.

Neither had Elias.

At times he had questioned if he was a good doctor or there by default.

He had, of course, had the very best education at a top English boarding school.

And after his time in the military he had studied medicine at Oxford.

Everything had been, his friends had ribbed him at times, handed to him on a plate.

Tonight Elias had found out that he was a doctor.

A real one.

And a very good one at that, because somehow he'd just shoved his personal torment aside.

Delivering a premature infant when it wasn't your specialty was scary at best.

But delivering that infant when you were sure it was your baby had had his heart racing so fast it had surely matched the baby's rate at times.

Having then to tear himself away, having to focus on work when everything precious to him was in that room had proved agony.

Yet Elias knew that the neonatologist, even if he received a devastating personal call, would carry on working on the baby until a replacement arrived.

That was the position he had found himself in.

Oh, had Elias declared a personal interest in these two patients then the staff might have understood him stepping back.

But that would have helped no one tonight so he had pushed through as best he could.

His head felt as if it was exploding and he felt sick in his guts as he walked into Resus, where a mother was sobbing as her two-year-old convulsed.

Elias gave that two-year-old his focus.

He administered the right medication and asked all the right questions.

'He was sick last night when he went to bed,' the child's mother said. 'I thought that it was just a cold…'

'He has a very high fever,' Elias told her.

The little boy had stopped convulsing and now lay crying and confused as Elias sat down on the resuscitation bed.

'Hello,' he said to the little boy, who was disoriented and fretful. 'Your mum is here…' He nodded for her to come around the bed so that the little boy could see her. 'My name is Elias, I'm a doctor at the hospital…' And then he said what was important again. 'Your mum is here.'

And he needed to be over there.

With *his* baby's mum.

Yet he thoroughly examined the child, carefully looking at his throat and ears and listening to his chest.

He did what he had to do.

He was peripherally aware that his baby had been transferred because as Valerie came into Resus to get some equipment the doors had opened and he had seen an incubator being wheeled out.

He took some bloods and then filled out the forms for the blood work and ordered a chest X-ray for the child as he thought that he might have pneumonia.

And then he went to speak with the paediatrician but when he saw Roger, Elias asked if he could have a word.

'I've just been informed about a family emergency,' Elias told him.

Roger could see how pale Elias was and didn't doubt that he was struggling to hold it together. 'I'll call in Raj,' Roger said immediately.

He picked up the phone and did just that. 'He's on his way but it might be half an hour until he arrives.'

Elias nodded. 'Thanks.'

He would have to stay until Raj got there.

The department was busy and Elias could not wait idly. He went and examined an overdose case that had just arrived.

He mixed up some activated charcoal for the patient to drink but then he saw Mandy running through an IV.

'How's the baby?' he asked, and she made a wobbly gesture with her hand.

'They sped her off to St Patrick's.'

'And how's the mother?'

'She went in a separate ambulance. Poor woman, she was down in London for work. It must be terrifying to be so far from home.'

Mandy looked at Elias and saw his grey complexion. 'I'm sorry to hear that you've had bad news but you'll still have to fill out paperwork for them before you go. They'll need a number for the baby.'

'Sure,' Elias said, because the little girl would need to be added to the system quickly as she had been transferred to another hospital.

He gave the overdose the activated charcoal to drink. Her boyfriend was with her and Elias explained the importance of finishing the bottle.

'It looks awful, I know,' he said, 'but it doesn't really taste of anything. Make sure she drinks it all. Any problems, press this bell. The medics should be down soon to admit her.'

Elias moved to the nurses' station and took out the other paperwork that was waiting to be filled in.

Elizabeth Foster.

He saw that she was now twenty-three and

that she lived in Edinburgh, though when he had met her Beth had lived in Dunroath, a small fishing village on the east coast of Fife.

And she had put Rory as her next of kin.

He knew that was her ex.

Maybe they were back together?

Perhaps the baby wasn't even his.

Elias knew that she was, though, and not just from the dates.

Beth had made a comment on the night they had met about being a 'daughter of the manse'.

He hadn't known what it had meant then.

He knew what it meant now—her father was a minister and very strict.

Elias guessed that these past months would have pretty much been hell for her.

He wrote up his patient notes.

Presented to Accident and Emergency department at 29/40 gestation.

And he wrote about the rapid delivery and all that had happened and that she had been transferred to St Patrick's for postnatal care.

And then he went to the other patient that required a signature.

There were rather a lot of forms to fill in when it came to a new life.

Baby Foster.
Born 29/40 weeks gestation.
Precipitate labour, rapid delivery.
One-minute Apgar score: 7

His hand was shaking as he wrote because the ramifications were just starting to hit him.

Not just that he had become a father.

The second in line to the throne had just delivered the third in line to the throne.

The palace always announced the delivering doctor.

He could see the headlines and the chaos the press would make of the circumstances tonight.

All this he was starting to envision but not quite, because all he could really see in his mind's eye was the sight of the baby. Her tiny head and flaccid limbs. The little tufts of red hair and that she had been struggling to breathe. How her eyes had closed and her nostrils had flared as her tiny mouth had blown bubbles.

What the hell was he doing here?

Elias was closer to tears than he had ever been in his life and panic was building as he placed his head in his hands.

'Are you okay?' Roger checked.

He too knew how hard it was to work when you had just been informed of a personal crisis.

'Not really,' Elias said, and he took a steadying breath and told himself that Beth and the baby were in good hands—but he needed to see that for himself.

Then came the words that he had waited to hear.

'Raj is here.'

'Thank you.'

The department was covered.

Elias walked briskly around to the on-call room and pulled off his scrubs and runners and changed into black jeans and a jumper and pulled on his boots and jacket.

Then he turned off the white-noise machine and walked out.

The man was still singing 'I Belong to Glasgow' as he walked through the observation room and then stepped out of the fire exit and into the night.

His baby would belong to Medrindos.

If he told his family what was happening huge wheels would be set in instant motion. There would be lawyers and background checks immediately commenced on Beth. He would be told to step back and let the palace handle things from here.

A princess had just been born and Beth didn't even know that he was royal.

Elias had chosen not to tell her that night.

He knew it was his baby.

Not because of some instant connection or primal instinct that the child was his.

But because he had got to know Beth that night.

Whatever the palace or her family might make of their encounter, no matter how they might deem it a one-night stand, he knew what a rare gift it had been.

For both of them.

CHAPTER FOUR

IT HAD ALL gone perfectly.

George and Voula Costas had just celebrated their twenty-fifth wedding anniversary on the Greek island where they had grown up and married.

The surprise party had been organised by Beth.

Months of preparation had come together and as Beth walked into her villa and closed the door behind her she was smiling as she kicked off her sandals.

The waiter had sent her home with a large cocktail in a plastic glass and she was looking forward to simply unwinding after an exhausting couple of days.

It was a hot night and she turned the fan on above her bed. She peeled off the smart linen shift dress she had worn tonight and let down her hair, shaking it loose, happy with how the night had gone.

She was just about to lie down when the phone rang.

She had known that it would soon ring.

It would be her father, calling to check how the night had gone. Or rather he would use that as an excuse to check she was safely home.

For a moment Beth had considered not answering it.

She was twenty-two years old after all.

England was two hours behind Greece and she could imagine her father pacing and waiting to make the call. If she didn't answer, he and her mother would stress and try again. It was easier all round to answer, and, she told herself, it was no big deal, so she picked up the receiver.

'Hi, Dad,' Beth said.

'How did you know it was me?' Donald sounded surprised.

She could have answered that it had to be him because it was too late for Housekeeping and anyone else would have called her on her mobile!

Of course her father would say it was too expensive to make an international call on the mobile but Beth knew he had called her on the landline to check she was safely in for the night.

'Just a good guess,' Beth answered as she rolled her eyes.

She tried not to be cross. After all, it was her first time overseas and she had recently broken up with her long-term boyfriend, Rory, which had caused a lot of upset all around.

'Your mother and I just wanted to know how the night went. Was Voula surprised?'

'She certainly was.'

'You don't think she'd guessed what George was planning?'

'No.' Beth shook her head and found she was smiling. 'She really didn't have a clue.'

They chatted for a few moments and Beth actually enjoyed doing so.

Her father knew the Costases and many of the people who had attended tonight. While he might not be happy that his daughter was overseas, it didn't mean that he wasn't interested in how things had gone.

The call ended very amicably and Beth lay on the bed but the happy buzz that had followed her into the villa had dispersed.

She loved her parents a lot but she felt stifled by them.

Her father was a minister and, growing up, it had never proven much of a problem for Beth.

She'd had a wonderful childhood.

Seriously wonderful.

She was an only child and had been a late arrival into her parents' lives. The manse where they lived was a happy home and had a constant flow of visitors. They often had guests from overseas stay with them, which Beth especially loved. Holidays had been spent exploring rugged beaches or camping, and her father's position in the village hadn't been an issue then.

Oh, she'd been warned, many times, that her actions reflected on her father and that she was to always behave. But, even during teenage years, her strict upbringing hadn't been much of an encumbrance. Beth had enjoyed school and there had always been something to do in the evenings and at weekends.

She'd loved to read and her friends occasionally slipped her books that would have caused the most terrible row had they been found.

They hadn't been found, though.

She'd had a close circle of friends and as for boys, possibly had she been taken with anyone there might have been a clash, but she hadn't been particularly attracted to anyone.

Oh, there had been the occasional stand-off between her and her parents. Beth was stubborn and her temper matched her hair colour, and as a little girl she had fired up easily but she had learnt to choose her battles.

It was as she'd entered adulthood that the problems had started and small whispers of discontent had made themselves known.

In her final year of school her parents had steered her towards nursing or maybe teaching.

Beth had been excited at the prospect of studying in Edinburgh and had been hoping to share a flat with her great friend Shona.

Her father had had other ideas.

There was a close colleague of his who had been more than happy to offer her board, and naturally she would come home during the holidays and on weekends and days off.

A big row had ensued when Beth had stated she wanted to share a flat with her friend. But in the months that had followed Beth had realised that it wasn't nursing or teaching she really wanted.

They had been a chance to leave home and that didn't seem a very sensible reason to make a career choice.

And so she had fought to pursue the career she now loved but she still lived at home.

It was nice to get away.

Beth climbed off the bed and walked to the window, but before she pulled back one of the shutters she wrapped herself in a sarong she had bought at a market.

The night was beautiful.

The sky was a deep navy and so too was the Mediterranean. There was a riot of stars and a small sliver of moon and she could see the trees swaying in the stiff breeze.

On the water a stunning yacht was lit up and there were smaller boats around it. There had been great excitement from the locals about some young royals sailing in.

She could hear the celebrations continuing next door and suddenly Beth wanted to be out there.

Not to party, more to walk and just revel in this rare night of freedom.

She went to her drawer and pulled out a grey tube dress that she had bought at the same market where she had got the sarong.

Both she would leave behind as they wouldn't be considered suitable back home.

The dress clung to her and showed her slender shape and the curve of her hips and bust. It wasn't short but it came above her knee and showed a lot more skin than she usually would. She had no cleavage to speak of but the scoop of the dress almost gave her one.

It was plain, it was comfortable, it was a little tight and it was subtly sexy.

Beth picked up a hair tie but then decided to wear it down. She didn't even bother with sandals.

Instead, she picked up the cocktail that had been made for her and headed out of the villa. She could go and join in the party, Mr Costas wouldn't mind at all—in fact, he'd be pleased to see her.

She just wasn't in the mood to party.

She wanted to think.

Away from work, away from the manse, and now out of her relationship with Rory, Beth needed to work out what she wanted to do with her life.

The beach beckoned and Beth crossed the road and stepped onto the soft cool sand and walked for a while.

She could hear laughter and music coming from the yacht.

She chose to sit under one of the swaying palms and selected her spot on the deserted beach.

And it was then that she first saw him.

Beth had only idly watched at first as a shadow had moved along the pier.

He was a good distance away and walking along the beach but every now and then he would turn and look out to the ocean. The closer he got, the more he intrigued her. He was tall and broad shouldered and there was a certain elegance to him. His profile was strong and as he stopped near Beth, she knew she hadn't been seen.

He looked pensive as he looked out over the water and there was just something about him that made her want to know more. He took the bottle he was carrying and deftly dealt with the cork. Hearing the pop, Beth found herself smiling, though she held back from making herself known.

Then again, wasn't that what she always did?

Or, rather, what she had always been told to do—hold herself back.

'Celebrating?' Beth asked.

He turned, clearly a little taken aback that someone was there.

'I guess I am,' he said. He looked at her plastic glass and held up the bottle and Beth's smile widened.

'I thought you'd never ask.'

They chatted a little and then he said, 'I'm Elias.' There was a moment when they could either get back to their own worlds or spend a while finding out about each other.

Her father would freak if he knew that she patted the sand beside her in invitation for Elias to take a seat.

Then again her father would freak if he knew his twenty-two-year-old daughter was sitting drinking champagne with a man on a beach after midnight.

'I'm Beth.' She told him her name as he joined her. 'So, why the champagne?'

'Why not?' he asked, smiling at her soft Scottish accent. 'Are you here on holiday?'

'I am now!' She nodded. 'I was actually here for work but as of fifteen minutes ago I'm officially on holiday.'

Hence the cocktail, hence the tiny victory salute to herself that she had made it through three pretty grim months.

'What work do you do?' he asked.

'I'm an events co-ordinator,' Beth told him, and gestured with her head in the direction of the hotel behind them.

There was laughter and music coming from there as well as from the yacht.

'I've spent the last few months trying to organise a surprise twenty-fifth wedding anniversary.'

'Twenty-five years!' Elias said, and the wry edge to his voice told her his jaded view on the topic.

'I thought the same but their marriage and the way that they've celebrated it has taught me a thing or two.'

'Such as?'

She gave a small shake of her head, not wanting to reveal the very personal lessons that had been learnt. 'What do you do for work?' she asked him, and it was Elias who now hesitated.

He didn't want to tell her his royal status.

It tended to change things and, right now, he didn't want to change a thing. 'I'm a doctor.'

'Do you enjoy it?'

He had. 'Very much.'

'What made you want to study medicine?'

'It just interested me and…' He had never really discussed it. 'It seemed a worthwhile career.' That was the best way he could describe it. When he was working, he had felt as if he was doing something worthwhile.

'It is,' Beth said, and then smiled. 'I was supposed to be a nurse.'

'Supposed to be?' Elias checked.

'It's a *respectable* profession.'

'Of course it is.' Elias frowned. He was just starting to get a handle on her accent but suddenly it became more pronounced and it took a moment to register that she was perhaps impersonating someone.

She was! Beth was remembering the time she had first suggested she make a career as an events co-ordinator. It had made perfect sense.

Nearly every week there was a new bride-to-be coming through the manse.

'Ask Beth,' her father would say, when the bride wanted to know about reception venues.

In summer there might be two weddings or more at a weekend, and Beth had known from experience the numbers that the various restaurants housed.

And she hadn't just helped with weddings but christenings too, so she had broached the idea to her father about making a career out of it.

'You want to *charge* for helping to organise a celebration?' Donald frowned. 'You want to make a living out of it?' He had sounded appalled.

'Well, you do,' Beth had answered.

'Elizabeth,' her mother, Jean, had warned.

Her lips had shuttered and pinched and usually at this point Beth would flounce off, only on this day she had chosen to stand up for the career she'd now badly wanted.

'But it's true,' Beth had insisted. 'Why shouldn't I make a living doing something I enjoy, something I am good at and passionate about?'

It had caused a huge row, their first real confrontation, as at eighteen years old she had stood her ground.

Now her business was not thriving exactly but it was doing well.

But, no, her father didn't consider it to be a decent profession for a single woman.

'And an events co-ordinator isn't respectable?' Elias asked.

'Apparently not.' She didn't explain how hard she had fought to make this her profession and that tonight was a serious highlight. Her father hadn't wanted her to travel overseas but Beth had put her foot down and said that she was quite old enough to make that decision for herself. After weeks liaising with the hotel and guests, it had been incredibly satisfying to see it all come together tonight.

'I've loved organising the party. Mr Costas has a couple of restaurants back home—one in Dunroath, where I'm from, and now one in Edinburgh. I organised the opening night for the Edinburgh one and then he asked me to help with his wedding anniversary. You should have seen the expression on his wife's face when she walked into the hotel restaurant. At first she thought it was a coincidence that there was a table with some of her friends and then she looked around...' Beth saw that he was smiling as she described what had taken place. 'She realised that the whole place was filled with friends and relatives. She'd thought she was just on holiday with her husband…'

'Was it hard to organise?'

'It was.' Beth nodded. 'I had a lot going on in my personal life at the time.'

'Such as?' Elias asked, and reached for the champagne and filled her glass.

His question was direct but now it didn't faze her.

'I broke up with my boyfriend. We'd been together a long time.' She stared out to the sea and heard carefree laughter that came from the hotel behind and the yacht ahead.

It no longer matched her mood.

'He was a really nice man,' Beth said. 'Everyone thought we were about to get engaged.'

And it had hurt to end things.

It hadn't hurt enough, though, and she found herself explaining that to Elias.

'I was listening to Mr Costas and all the ways in which he wanted to surprise his wife. How, even after a quarter of a century together, he was still excited at the prospect of making her happy. I would watch him take a call from her and his face would light up…'

It had been a huge awakening as she'd realised she didn't feel that way about Rory.

'We started going out when I was eighteen.'

'How old are you now?'

'Twenty-two.'

'Four years!' Elias said. 'I think the most I've managed is…' He thought for a moment and then shook his head. 'I don't really keep count but I'd be lucky to run into four weeks… that really is a long time.'

'Not really…'

She didn't explain how strict her father was. How the first year had been a coffee in the church hall after the service on Sunday. The second year they had graduated to a meal at the weekend and then he would see her home.

And she certainly didn't tell Elias how Rory had understood her strict upbringing and had been completely prepared to wait until they were married to do anything more than kiss.

She didn't tell Elias how that had horrified her.

That she didn't want to wait.

And so they hadn't.

Yet, though Beth had longed for furtive sexy kisses and snatched times together, it had been far gentler on the senses than Beth had hoped it would be. It was passion that had been missing. Though she cared for him it hadn't been exciting or breathtaking; instead, it had been safe and kind and…

Beth struggled to find the word in her head and then came to it—adequate.

'He's such a nice man, I can't really justify it, except...' Beth gave a helpless shrug and there were tears in her eyes, Elias saw, and he understood her.

Oh, he and Sophie hadn't so much as danced, let alone been together for four years, but he did understand that Beth hadn't wanted to settle.

'He told me that he was going to speak to my father.'

Elias frowned.

'To ask for my hand in marriage,' Beth explained.

'Oh!'

'My parents are really strict, there was no question of us moving in together. It probably sounds odd.'

'Not really.'

He thought of his parents, the King and Queen of Medrindos, and how they'd take to the suggestion that he move in with someone.

'I'm a daughter of the manse,' Beth said, and when he frowned again she didn't fully explain but she made things a little clearer. 'The only way I get to leave home is in a coffin or a wedding gown.'

'I get it.'

He put a hand over hers and it startled Beth. Nicely so.

Not just that the contact was a touch more brazen than she was used to but more the way his hand felt over hers.

Hot and dry, his fingers closed around hers and remained there.

It had taken Rory six months to even get to that.

'They didn't even want me to come here,' Beth said.

'But here you are!'

'And I'm very glad to be.'

She was.

Especially now.

He was easy to talk to and Beth could talk!

Perhaps it was because it was dark and she knew he couldn't see that she was blushing. He was incredibly attractive and usually that would have her tongue in knots.

Not tonight.

'So,' he asked her, 'do you speak Greek?'

'Not a word.' Beth laughed.

'How did you organise it?'

'Thankfully the people I liaised with spoke English, and if they didn't they found someone who did, although my accent was a bit of a barrier.'

'I like it,' he said. It was lyrical and he liked that he had to think a little if she spoke too fast.

Now she asked about him. 'So, are you here on holiday?'

'Yes.'

That wasn't a lie. Lately his life had been just one long holiday as he'd partied hard before he inevitably settled down.

'When do you fly back?' Elias asked her.

'Monday,' Beth sighed. It had all gone by too soon. 'Tomorrow I just have to make sure the hotel's happy and that everyone's been paid and then the afternoon and evening are mine. What about you?'

'I leave in the morning.'

The yacht sailed off at midday for Medrindos. There was an official function tomorrow night that the Princes had to attend and, no doubt, he was going to walk straight back into an argument, given that again he and Sophie had stayed apart.

That left them with tonight.

It didn't seem long enough.

'Do you want to find a club?' he offered. 'Dance?'

'I can't dance.'

'I bet you can.'

'Nope.' She smiled and then she admitted something. 'I wanted to have dance lessons.'

'But you didn't?'

'No.' Beth sighed as she thought about all the things she hadn't been allowed to do.

She looked up at the stars and was perfectly content to stay where they were rather than go to some club.

'Is it always this beautiful here?' Beth asked.

It was always this beautiful, Elias guessed. The difference was it *felt* beautiful tonight.

But then he heard the buzz of his phone and as he sat up to retrieve it Beth guessed their time together was about to conclude.

She was pleasantly surprised when, instead of checking who it was, Elias switched his phone off and put it beside the now empty champagne bottle. 'Nowhere you need to be?' Beth checked.

'Not yet.' He lay down on the sand and looked up at the sky. 'You?'

She hesitated before shaking her head. Now was the ideal time to make an excuse and head in.

Beth didn't want to, though.

And so she lay down too.

The party at the hotel was wrapping up and now the noise from the yacht was clearer.

There was music drifting across the water and right now he should be dancing with Sophie.

He hadn't wanted to, though.

He looked over at Beth. He could see her little pointy nose and that her long curls moved in the breeze.

'Are you a redhead?' he asked, because the moon was just a sliver but every now and then he got a glimpse of muted reddish gold.

'I am,' Beth said, and turned her head so they faced each other.

'What colour are your eyes?' he asked while staring deep into them.

'Blue,' Beth answered. 'What about yours?'

'Grey,' Elias said. 'And my hair's black.'

'I can see that.'

And she could see the shadows of his cheekbones and a lovely full mouth.

He could have kissed her then.

Elias read women well and the easiest thing in the world would be to lean over a little and yet there was something else he wanted to do, and only with Beth. And so, instead of kissing her, he stood. He took out his wallet and added it to his phone that lay beside the champagne bottle and she looked up at him and then smiled when he held out his hand.

'Do you want to dance?'

CHAPTER FIVE

BETH WANTED TO DANCE.

More so than she ever had in her life.

She put her villa key beside the little pile they had made and took his hand. He pulled her up to a stand.

He was far taller than she had realised because now that they were both standing he towered over her.

And he was broad.

All these little details she took in as still he held her hand and led her not to a dance floor but to the water's edge.

Still he held her hand but he held it up now and the other arm went to her waist.

'I can't dance,' she told him.

'Of course you can.' He raised their hands higher and she twirled but stumbled.

'I really can't dance,' she told him.

He let her twirl again and she laughed and then he brought her into him and he told her where to put her feet. He really knew what he was doing, Beth realised. '*You* can dance!'

He surprised her.

As she'd walked to the water she'd thought it had been just a smooth line and that it would be a little sway against each other he might have in mind, a sway that would lead to a kiss.

And she'd have taken that.

Now, though, they danced.

And he could dance, which meant so too could she.

'I always wanted to learn how to tip back and be caught...'

He laughed. 'It's called a dip.'

All those hours upon hours of formal dance lessons that he'd loathed at the time were suddenly worth it for this.

He spun her in and put his hand on her back. He explained how to do it but every time she tried to lean back Beth went rigid.

'I can't.'

She tried a couple of times but she simply could not fall back.

'It's my job not to drop you,' he said. 'I shan't.'

He pulled her into him and they were a breath away from a kiss. She could feel the thump-thump of his heart against her chest and she looked at his mouth as he spoke.

'We could try in the water.'

Now he watched as her mouth moved into a slow smile. 'That's a terrible excuse to get me undressed.'

'I don't make excuses.'

And, instead of stripping down, he took her hand and they ran into the shallows. The water felt cool as they waded in dressed.

'Is that why you took out your wallet?' she asked, wrapping her arms around his neck and wanting her kiss. 'You knew that we'd end up in the water?'

'No,' he said.

'I don't believe you,' she said, and she no longer wanted to just dance. She was accustomed to the water now and could feel the pull of it around her thighs and the steadiness of his hands on her hips.

'Believe me,' he said.

She did.

He kissed her then and it was slow but not soft.

No, it was not soft or tentative, as she had been used to. It was truly like being kissed for the first time. In fact, it was far better than being kissed for the first time, because his tongue was expert and matched her need.

There had always been need in Beth and it

had never once been properly met, but it was starting to be now.

Her hands went to his hair and her fingers knotted and she kissed him back. Her tongue was suggestive and the best part—his was more so.

This was how a kiss should be, Beth thought as he pulled her in tighter to his body.

She could feel him harden and, unlike a certain other, he did not move his hips back in an attempt to disguise it; instead, he moved her in tighter for a better feel. The water felt cool compared to the heat between her legs. Still he held her hips and then he pulled back his mouth and she watched as he moved his tongue over his lips as if tasting her again while his erection nudged her.

She was more than a little bit breathless and, as she stared back at him, Beth revised her choice of the word adequate.

Elias's kiss was the most inadequate kiss she had ever had but in the most delicious way. Each caress, each stroke of his tongue remained adequate for but a second and then rapidly diminished to woefully inadequate for it made her crave more.

She moved her mouth back to his but he pulled his head back.

'We're here to dance.'

What a dance.

They were both turned on and now when she leant back into his palm he was upright and steady.

It didn't end there, though, he brought her back up gently.

'Again,' Beth said.

And he twirled her into him and then put his hand in her back to signal she would be dipped and she lowered more deeply until her hair trailed in the water as he swept her back up to his arms.

'Again,' she said.

And she went back again and again.

She got drenched but it didn't matter because as he pulled her back up she leant into him.

They were breathless, but not just from exertion.

Standing in the shallows, she tasted his salty neck as his hands came between them and stroked her breasts through her dress. She kissed his ear and realised she'd never kissed an ear before. Neither had she heard such a low growl or felt fingers move down and dig hard into her bottom.

She lifted her eyes and they stared at each other and without a word walked to shore.

The sand made their legs feel suddenly heavy.

'One more try,' Beth said, because they had not tried their dance move on land.

And he almost let her fall, but caught her in time, and then he did let her fall gently and met her on the sand.

There were kisses and there were kisses and then there was this. She was wet, turned on, fully dressed, and he was to the side of her, leaning over. He kissed her harder and rougher than she could ever have imagined and it tasted divine.

He felt the thrum of her passion, like an orchestra tuning, and frantic outbursts that needed to be honed and so he kissed her in a way he usually didn't.

Kissing tended to bore him but not this time—he was the expert conductor she had never known, reading the beats of her body and the building moans and then the unexpected feel of her resistance.

For Beth there was a brief moment of certainty that she could not kiss like this for long. 'We need to stop...' she breathed as she pulled her mouth away.

He was half on top of her, his erection pressed into her, and his mouth was driving her insane.

'Why?'

And so she told him. 'Or I'll come.'

'Isn't that what kissing's for?'

Not in her world.

Actually, not usually in his but he wanted to make her come right here, right now.

He kissed her hard and dirty, he probed her with his tongue and pressed his erection harder into her thigh.

It was amazing for Beth, her fingers knotted in his hair. Had her mouth not been full of his she would have sworn, which was something she never did.

Inadequate, there was that word again because she wanted him on top of her and for him to be inside her.

She ached for it, she was coming to the thought of it.

Her thighs were shaking and her hips wanted to rise, she wanted to pull him on top of her and to feel his solid weight.

And Elias felt every shiver and tasted her tension and the moan she made in his mouth. He swallowed and pressed himself into her hip but then he stopped, because he had to.

'Nearly,' he said, and she let out a shocked laugh as he dropped contact and leant up on his elbow.

This was what she had craved and what had been missing till now.

He looked down and watched her, eyes

closed, lips parted, trying to catch her breath, and then she opened her eyes to him and said, 'Come back to mine…'

about lips, parted. It sent to crush her breasts
and then she opened her eyes for a moment and
came back to mind.

CHAPTER SIX

SHE WAS OVERTAKEN with lust in a way she had never even come close to before.

He stood and helped her up and they walked over to where they had been sitting.

He picked up his wallet and phone and the empty champagne bottle and Beth took her plastic cup and key.

They tidied up after themselves.

Beth was nervous as they made their way to her villa—she had never done anything like this in her life. It was thrilling, it was exhilarating and it was everything that had been missing to date.

Beth had wanted to feel like this for a very, very long time.

It wasn't Elias who dragged her over to the hotel, protesting, it was the heat between her legs that guided her.

Oh, they nearly ran across the road and to the villa complex.

She opened the door and they stepped into her bedroom and he *must* downgrade more often, Elias thought, because were they in his usually luxury suite they wouldn't be two steps from the bed.

She went for his mouth but then, for Beth, Elias did the sexiest thing ever.

He turned on the lights.

Such a small detail but it meant the world to her. Always sex had been cloaked in guilt. She'd asked Rory to take her from behind once and the look he had given her had suggested she needed counselling. It had always been an under-the-covers procedure that required her imagination to wander if satisfaction was to be gained.

Her imagination was put on ice tonight.

Elias saw the absolute state they were in.

Her glorious auburn hair looked as if it had had concrete poured on it, his black trousers wore half the beach and so too did her dress.

In her villa he took charge and walked them to the tiny shower.

Had it been left to Beth, she would have peeled off her dress and dealt with it in the morning.

Instead, he turned on the shower full blast and they went in clothed.

They kissed under it, pulled faces at the

sandy grit that slipped into their mouths at times but didn't care in the least. He peeled off her dress and sure enough there was sand on her puckered nipples, which he washed away.

Her skin was so pale it was almost translucent. All of her was pale, from her pink nipples to pale blue veins, and he reddened her breasts with his lips and tongue.

Each freckle deserved attention, but he would be there till the middle of next week if he tried and so he got back to her mouth.

She stripped him of his shirt and soaped his arms and then chest and, because she wanted to, dressed in her panties, she turned him around and soaped his muscular back as Elias removed his trousers and underwear and hung them over the edge.

His buttocks were taut and she soaped them and slipped her hand between his thighs and she was absolutely the woman she had always been tonight—she had just never let herself be her before.

Then he turned and Beth's upper teeth bit her bottom lip. Naked his body was magnificent. He was long limbed but muscular, and there was a smattering of dark hair over his chest, not that she looked for very long. Neither did she properly take in his long thighs or flat stomach. She was looking at the lovely forbidden part and it was hard and angry-looking.

For her.

She soaped him, long and slow as he peeled off her panties.

It was all slow and sexy till then but the sight of her was his undoing.

He let out a sexy curse as he pulled down her knickers.

And it should've made her eyes bulge to be sworn at like that. Yet he was staring at her sex as if he'd never seen one.

Actually, Elias hadn't.

Well, not one quite so fiery red.

While he might have unknowingly slept with several redheads, they had been strawberry blondes by the time Elias had bedded them and downstairs had been bald and waxed.

Beth's mother had no idea that the little scissors in her sewing basket were put to an occasional other use.

Oh, Beth was so glad of that use now because she was neat and tidy and about to be so dirty for him.

He checked for sand. Every crevice he checked with his fingers and she almost slipped over, her legs were shaking so much.

Yes, she was his undoing because Elias turned off the taps and they just exploded to the other. He kissed her hard and lifted her and Beth wrapped her legs around him as he took her to the bed and dropped her on it.

She went to pull back the covers and climb in.

'Don't you dare,' he said.

In fact, he turned on the bedside lights too.

Beth lay there naked and watched his dark eyes roam over her. Every freckle shivered to his gaze and he climbed on the bed and knelt over her.

He kissed down her chest and teased her breast with feather-light strokes of his tongue. Then he climbed over her so that he knelt between her thighs and stroked her with his shaft.

She was up on her elbows, watching him, as he answered an earlier question. 'I left my wallet by the champagne so I didn't do you on the beach.'

'Oh.'

'I'll go and get it.'

The bastard was on the bathroom floor.

'In a moment,' Beth said.

Her face was flushed and so too her chest, and her hands came down and they both stroked him.

'Beth.' His voice was stern, but it was more that he was trying to reason with himself.

You would think, given the scandal that never was, it would be at the top of his mind to be careful, yet nothing had happened between that woman and him.

Might as well be hung for a sheep, Elias thought. His mind wasn't moving in its usual direction, he only cared now for now.

Elias watched as he slowly nudged in.

And Beth moaned as he started to fill her and her throat went tight as he pulled back and then he went in deeper.

He was so slow and measured and on his knees that as he started to thrust, something that felt like anger grew in her chest, a tension that built as it did when she held onto her temper. It made her teeth grit and her fingers ball into her palms.

'Elias,' she said, but it was in a cross voice that surprised her.

'What?' He smiled—it didn't surprise him in the least, he knew he was holding back.

'Elias!'

He stopped his slow thrusts then and moved her hips instead and she dropped from her elbows to her back and she felt as if she might cry as slowly he moved her. It was bliss but not deep enough.

It was odd, it was as if he exposed every held-in emotion but also he accepted her.

And then she said it.

Two words she'd never thought she would.

The words she had held back on the beach.

She asked him to take her, rather more rapidly than he was doing, and Beth expressed herself less than politely.

'I thought you'd never ask,' he said, and then suddenly, very suddenly, he obliged.

She felt the crush of his weight as he toppled onto her and then the crush of his mouth.

And then, just when she felt it could not get better, he got up on his elbows and the look he gave her was so intense as he did as she'd asked.

She had never known anything like it, neither had she ever heard the sound of really good sex.

He moaned and *he* shouted and when she pressed her hand to his mouth he removed it and held her wrist up high and angled himself better.

This elegant, pensive man was now unleashed and it made her shiver on the inside; it was raw and powerful and consuming and Beth let out a scream.

As he shot into her, it felt as if every cell in her body shrank in on itself and tightened. She was lost, almost unaware of the slowing in motion and the taste of his kiss, and then the sound of someone in the next villa knocking on the wall.

She laughed.

He did too.

They lay on their sides and faced each other and both gave a small delighted, guilty laugh as to the heights of their pleasure.

'Thank you…' he said, and Elias meant it.

Absolutely they were high.

And then she breathed and blinked in confusion.

Her first time and Rory had said 'Sorry' when he had come.

This man had thanked her.

'That was amazing,' Beth said, and she lay and faced him and then she looked down at his mouth and then back to his eyes. 'Aren't you going to kiss me goodnight?'

'No,' Elias said, and she liked his slow, lazy smile. 'You're going to kiss me.'

And she did.

With him it was all so easy to be herself.

Waking up was the only hard part of their time together.

Elias looked over to where she slept and the easiest thing in the world would be to just go back to sleep.

Or wake her with a kiss.

He got up and turned on his phone and checked the time. It was almost ten and that was a surprise in itself because he never overslept. He saw the many missed calls and texts, and the warning that he needed to get back.

There was a message from Alvera, telling him to contact her urgently.

No doubt to ask why nothing had happened between himself and Sophie.

He had only delayed the inevitable, Elias knew. Soon he would be officially engaged. He wanted Beth's number, he wanted to know about the woman he had met last night, but that would be cruel to both of them.

They could go nowhere, Elias knew.

He sat on the bed beside her and looked at her amazing red hair all wild on the pillow, and the last thing he wanted to do was walk away.

There was no choice, though.

Beth had never been woken by a kiss before.

It was so sexy and dreamy and right.

She ran her hands over his back and felt his damp shirt and then when she opened her eyes she knew this was goodbye.

'I have to go.' His forehead was on hers.

'I know.'

'We didn't use anything...'

'I'll be fine.'

He believed her. She'd been in a four-year relationship after all.

What he didn't know was that there had only been slow, cautious, occasional sex and, no, she certainly wasn't on the pill.

And what he didn't know was that there was no need to worry about other reasons for condom usage because with Beth and Rory's sexual history they'd be unlucky to even catch a cold.

And there she would also be okay because he was always careful.

Last night had been a delicious exception but duty now called.

He went to stand but her hands caught his and Beth looked at him. She didn't want him to go, in fact she wanted to ask for his number.

But what was the point?

Imagine her phone ringing back at the manse and her father asking who it was.

Perhaps she could invite him to tea!

She took a moment to look at him, to really look at him, all sexy and dishevelled and wearing damp clothes.

No, she could not imagine him taking tea at the manse and making polite small talk with her father.

Absolutely there was no hope for them.

'Thank you.'

It was her turn to say it to him now.

And at the time she meant it.

Elias had never found it more difficult to walk away from anyone but walk away he did.

He didn't accept any of Alvera's attempts to reach him.

There was a lot to think about and by the time he walked into the palace his mind was made up.

'I've given it a lot of thought and I've decided that I'm going back to medicine.' He met his mother's cool gaze. Alvera was in the office as well but Elias was more than used to that.

It was his father, Bruno, who responded. 'We've discussed this and you know it's not possible to practise here. You're a royal prince, it would be a nightmare for the hospital. As I've said, we can make a role for you—'

'I don't want a role to be made for me,' Elias said. 'I'm a doctor, that's what I do.'

He meant it. Elias had decided that he wasn't going back to Oxford, there were too many who knew he was royal there, but he could start again in London.

'Princess Sophie's family are never going to agree to that.' The King instantly dismissed it.

'I'm not marrying Sophie.'

Elias did not have a romantic bone in his body and, no, Beth was not on his mind when he said it. He just knew that he was nowhere near ready to settle down.

'Oh, so you want to carry on as you are, do you?' Queen Margarita said. 'Getting off with some commoner on the beach…'

She snapped her fingers and Alvera offered a sympathetic smile as she opened a file and handed him some photos. 'I tried to call you about it,' Alvera said.

He stared at the images.

They were actually very beautiful.

There was he and Beth dancing in the water, she was arched backwards, held by him, and her hair trailed in the water.

And there they were, kissing on the beach.

By Elias's standards these photos were tame but given all she had said about her parents and how strict they were…

Elias let out a breath. 'These can't get out.'

Alvera nodded. 'I'll do what I can. These were taken by the palace photographer. We're just hoping that there aren't any more.'

'Why did you have the palace photographer there?'

'Because,' Margarita answered for Alvera, 'we were hoping there might be some happy news to come from the palace for once, rather than yet another PR nightmare from one of my sons.'

'Well, it's happy news for me.' He went to stand but his father had other ideas.

'Elias,' his father snapped. 'We haven't finished. You can't just walk away, you have obligations…'

'And I'll fulfil the important ones' Elias said, and then he realised he had one very important obligation to fulfil right now, and he looked over at Alvera. 'You're to do everything to make sure no photos of last night get out.'

Unease was building and he took out his phone to check something.

'Elias!' His mother frowned at his insolence.

Not that he noticed.

Usually Elias walked away from women easily, yet he could recall every word of their conversation and he looked up one word he had not understood.

Manse.

And his heart plummeted when he saw that it was a house given to Scottish ministers.

Oh, Beth.

He went to walk out but then changed his mind and headed back to the desk, where he picked up the file that contained the photographs and shot them a warning.

'Never arrange to have me photographed without my express consent. I'm telling you now that if these ever get out you'll be explaining to your people why their Prince isn't back for birthdays, Christmas or anything...' His father started to speak but Elias overrode him. 'I'm serious,' he warned them.

He was.

Last night had been amazing.

He wanted nothing to spoil the memory.

For either of them.

CHAPTER SEVEN

THE MEMORY OF that night had twisted for Beth.

Her family's reaction to her pregnancy and the fact that she'd had a one-night stand had turned something beautiful and precious into something sordid.

She had been through a lot these past months. Finding out that she was pregnant, telling her parents, leaving home in disgrace and starting her career again almost from scratch while knowing she would soon have a baby to support.

None of that, though, compared to the fear of this—the uncertainty about whether her baby was at this minute alive.

No one could tell her anything.

Beth lay in a side room on the maternity ward and listened to the sound of crying babies, knowing that hers wasn't here—she had been taken straight to the NICU ward.

'Someone will come and speak with you as

soon as they are able to,' the midwife who admitted her had said.

Oh, they were kind and had settled her into bed and brought in a tray of tea and sandwiches, but they didn't know what was happening with her baby and that was the only thing Beth needed.

'She was having trouble breathing,' Beth said to another midwife when she came in and checked her blood pressure.

'Well, she's in the best place.'

And nobody could tell her anything.

'Can I go and see her?' Beth pleaded. 'I want to be with her.'

'Your blood pressure is very low and the medical staff are with her now. It won't help to have you there and fainting.'

And *still* nobody could tell her anything.

It was hell.

Left alone, Beth looked at the drip and was actually considering disconnecting it and finding her own way to NICU, that was how desperate she felt, but then she heard footsteps and she sat up, hoping for some news.

It was the receptionist who had come in earlier to ask some questions.

'There's an Elias Santini here, asking to see you.'

Beth lay back on the pillow. She didn't want

to see anyone other than a person who could tell her how her baby was, though she knew she had to face him.

'Can I send him in?' the receptionist checked.

Beth nodded and after a few moments heard heavy, swift footsteps coming toward her door. She turned her head and there he was, wearing black jeans and a heavy coat.

She'd forgotten how beautiful he was.

Beth had made herself forget just to survive.

Guilt and shame had distorted his features and sullied the memory of them and yet now here he was—Elias.

It had been necessary to forget, Beth realised, because otherwise she would have missed him so.

Unlike in Accident and Emergency, when he had seemed so calm and assured, she could see his tension and wondered if he was cross.

'I don't need this now…' she said.

'Beth.'

'I don't need you stomping in here and—'

'Nobody's stomping.'

Well, maybe he had been.

Elias now understood how accidents could happen as relatives raced to get to the department.

He had driven through wet London streets with adrenaline coursing through his veins and every traffic light had turned red as he had approached.

Thankfully, from working several shifts here he had a pass for the car park and had used it. Then he had raced through the hospital and to the maternity ward.

There it was dark and calm and, even with the sounds of babies crying, it was somehow peaceful, and as he had approached the desk a receptionist had smiled.

'Can I help you?'

'Beth Foster, she was just admitted…'

'And you are?'

Elias hadn't said he was the father.

Neither had he said that he was the doctor who had delivered the baby.

And certainly he hadn't been about to say that he was one of the Princes of Medrindos.

He had to work things out before any of that information was revealed.

'Elias Santini.'

'One moment.'

The receptionist had presumably gone to tell Beth that she had a visitor for she had returned a few moments later and told him that she was in Room Eleven and that it was straight down the corridor.

He was still full of adrenaline and had

fought not to run so, yes, perhaps he had stomped in.

'Have you heard how she is?' Elias asked.

'I haven't heard anything.' Beth shook her head. 'I just keep being told that someone will speak to me when they can or that my blood pressure is too low to go and wait up there...' She was trying not to break down and trying not to scream. 'I just want to go back to earlier...' It was hard to explain but she just wanted to still be pregnant. 'I just want to wake up and not to have had her. I don't know what I did wrong...'

'It's okay,' Elias said. 'You did nothing wrong. Sometimes these things just happen.'

Very rapid labours were traumatic and very confusing for the mother. Beth was incredibly pale and shivering and he was glad when a midwife came in and put another warm blanket over her.

She lay for a moment, taking in the warmth, and then she turned angry, accusing eyes on him. 'Before you accuse me of keeping it from you, I couldn't because you left without telling me your name.'

That had hurt.

The more she had thought about it over the months, the fact that he had left without giving any contact details had hurt her deeply.

'I know that.'

'Are you going to demand a DNA test?'

She watched as his eyes shuttered.

Certainly the palace would demand one.

Absolutely, before any discussion would take place it would be the first thing that would be requested.

He would be told to drop all communication with Beth and that the palace lawyers would take things from here, thank you very much. Alvera would be dispatched to handle all communications and warn Beth that it was in her best interests to stay quiet.

Beth didn't need all of that now.

And neither did he.

'We can talk about all that later,' he said.

'There's nothing to talk about.'

Oh, there was plenty but she was so angry at him.

Not for being here now but for leaving her then.

Yes, it had been by consent and just a one-night stand but the hurt had been immense and the repercussions intense and now she lay shocked and shivering and desperate for news about her baby.

'Let's just get through tonight,' Elias said.

'Can she, though?' Beth asked, and then panicked to have voiced her fears. 'There are babies born much earlier than that who do okay, aren't there?'

'Yes,' Elias said, but it was still very early and the baby would need a lot of help. He wanted to reassure her and also to reassure himself. 'Most babies born at this stage live…'

And then he stopped talking because he sounded like a statistician and this wasn't *most* babies and across the corridor, right now, his child was fighting just to breathe. 'She's in the best place,' he said.

'So I keep being told.' She felt as if ants were crawling over her skin. Beth physically itched to know how her baby was. 'Can you go up and say that you're a doctor…?'

That wouldn't mean anything, Elias knew. They weren't just going to let him in just because he was an Accident and Emergency doctor.

It would be entirely different if he said that he was the father.

Beth could not know the minefield he was walking through in his head. If it got back to the palace that he'd had a baby, the whole machine would swing into place. If the press found out that he had delivered his own baby…

Elias closed his eyes.

They had to keep it under wraps for now.

He opened his eyes to Beth.

'Tell them that I'm the father.'

Beth gave a low, mirthless laugh. 'You are!'

'I mean, we don't have to make it official…'

He watched as she frowned but he didn't further explain.

To register the birth in his name would be like sending a direct fax to every media outlet and the palace, but they didn't have to worry about that yet.

For now the priority was getting in to see the baby.

'Give me your phone number and when I know something I'll text you,' Elias offered. 'I can take a picture of her when I get in…'

She ached to know and, whether or not he believed her, Beth knew he was the father so she pressed the call bell.

'This is my daughter's father,' Beth said when the midwife came in. 'Can he go up to the NICU?'

'Of course,' the midwife said. 'I'll call and let them know that you're on the way.'

And she told him about the intercom system there and how he couldn't simply walk in and then she left them.

'I'll text you as soon as I hear anything,' he said. 'Though I'll probably just be sitting in a waiting room but at least…'

He didn't finish.

At least one of them would be close to her.
Beth nodded.

'Go.'

He had been right in his prediction—Elias
buzzed and was let in but was promptly shown
to a small waiting room.

He glanced at his phone.

He had her number now.

He just wished he'd had it all those months
ago and that she'd had his.

His phone bleeped.

Any news?

He was just about to text back and tell Beth
that there was nothing to report when there
was a knock on the door and a woman dressed
in scrubs came in.

She introduced herself as Cathy and said
that she was the senior nurse on tonight.

'We've had three emergency admissions
since midnight,' she explained. 'Your daughter and a set of twins, so it's going to be a
while until the neonatologist can come in and
speak with you.'

Elias nodded.

'Right now, your daughter is a little more
settled than she was when she first arrived.

She was having difficulty breathing and the decision was made to put her on CPAP,' Cathy explained. 'She's not ventilated, it's a form of positive air pressure to keep her airways open.'

Elias nodded and it was then that he said he was a doctor. 'Though this certainly isn't my speciality.'

'Well, at least you'll know some of what to expect,' Cathy said. 'She's had surfactant put down into her lungs and that will help with her breathing. She's quite a good size for twenty-nine weeks. Do you have exact dates?'

Elias was about to shake his head but then realised he did, in fact, have exact dates easily to hand.

He'd been there after all!

And they sat with a daisy wheel that worked out due dates and found out some good news.

'If you can be sure that that's the date of conception, it puts your daughter, as of today, at thirty weeks.'

Oh, that was good news.

Just that little nudge over the line and Elias blew out a breath as Cathy carried on speaking and told him they were in for quite a rollercoaster ride but that the staff were prepared for all that and would guide them as to what to expect.

'Would you like to see her?'

Elias nodded.

'Can I just call Beth and tell her what you've told me?'

She answered on first ring.

'I've just spoken with a nurse and I'm about to go in and see her.'

She didn't say anything at first and he could hear that she was crying.

'I'll come straight down and see you afterwards.'

'Can you tell her that I love her?'

'Of course.'

Cathy warned him how things would be but even with her careful explanations and even though he was a doctor, it was still a shock.

His daughter wasn't in an incubator and was still lying on a resuscitation cot with lights over her to keep her warm. She had on a little pink hat and nappy and there were tubes everywhere—she looked so exhausted and frail.

He could see the cord clip Mandy had applied but then she had been pink and vigorous.

Now she looked as if she'd washed up in the tide.

A NICU nurse gave him a smile but she was watching the baby carefully and it was Cathy who answered any questions that he had.

His baby lay with her limbs flaccid by her

sides and her eyes closed, and Elias thought his heart might break because he didn't even recognise her now.

Nearby the team were working frantically on the twins and there were staff everywhere but all he could see was his daughter.

'Can I touch her?' Elias asked.

'They like a firm touch,' Cathy explained. 'Put your hand on her head…' she guided one there '…and cup her little feet.'

He did so and it was like touching air.

And, yes, as he held her little head Elias was aware that he had made mistakes in his past and that the palace would presume her one of them.

Very possibly, though, she was the most perfect thing in his life but, yes, so very small and so fragile.

'I should take a photo for her mum…'

Everything felt strange, that he had a daughter, that Beth was a mum.

'I can do that for you,' Cathy said as the NICU nurse kept a second-by-second eye on her charge.

He moved his hands away so that she could get a clear photo of her for Beth and as he did, he took her little hand in his and stroked her palm and watched her little fingers go around his. It wasn't just beautiful to watch, it also made him breathe out in relief that she had that reflex, because she was so flaccid and still.

But then she opened her eyes. She had little almond-shaped eyes like her mother's and Elias felt his heart twist because he recognised her now and he lowered his head to be near hers.

'Mummy and Daddy love you.'

It sounded odd to Elias and yet it felt true, though it came from a place he did not know because he was still trying to fathom that he was a father.

And yet, when he was there, looking at her, it was all very, very simple.

'We love you very much,' he told her 'and we're going to sort this. We're going to do right by you. So, hang in there.'

And then he went down to see Beth.

He was more aware of the noise of his boots and tried not to startle her this time.

She was lying on her back and just staring at the ceiling and then her face turned.

'She's okay,' Elias said. 'She's beautiful.'

Beth burst into tears, she just dissolved, there wasn't even a moment to tell her about the photos or all that Cathy had said.

He just went over and sat on the bed and took her in his arms.

As if it was the completely normal thing to do.

And it was the right thing for Beth for it felt so good to be held by him.

Even if she was cross with him, scared, or rather terrified, it felt so good to be back in his arms and to know that he had seen their daughter and that for now her baby was okay.

For weeks, actually months, she hadn't been held.

There had been the occasional pat on her shoulder from a midwife or the odd handshake from a client.

To be wrapped now in a strong hug felt like a life jacket and she just leant against his chest as he told her all he had found out.

'There's some good news,' he told her. 'She's thirty weeks…'

Elias told her everything that had been told to him but very gently.

'I want to see her.'

'You will.'

It was then that he took out the phone, and the neonatal nurse had been busy.

There was a shot of her lying on her back with a little pink hat on.

'You can't wear pink if you have red hair.' Beth smiled through her tears. 'I'll have to tell them that.'

There were several and all she looked like was a premature baby with a lot of tubes. Beth just ached for a photo of the daughter she had so briefly held but this could be any baby.

And she felt terrible for thinking that.

Then she gasped because as Elias flicked through they came to a photo of her with her eyes open.

Then there was another with Elias crouched down and looking right at her.

'I was telling her how much you loved her,' he explained.

Then there was a photo of his finger and her tiny hand. That had, as of now, become his screensaver.

'Send them to my phone,' Beth said, and he did so.

'She's going to be okay,' Elias said, simply because she had to be.

'I just want her to have a normal healthy life.'

And he couldn't answer that.

He prayed that she was healthy but it would be a fight to give her even a semblance of a normal life.

She was a princess after all.

How, Elias pondered, when Beth was so overwhelmed and drained, did he slip into the conversation that she had just given birth to the third in line to the throne of Medrindos?

He didn't.

Quite simply, he could not land it all on Beth.

And neither would he tell his family, Elias decided.

It would either be handled discreetly as a mistake or they would be pushed to marry.

Even if he could persuade them that the baby was in the best place, there would be different doctors summoned, heightened security and bodyguards at the doors.

And as for the press…

No, he wanted a chance of normalcy for them.

There were weeks before the birth had to legally be registered.

Six weeks before the world found out about them and, Elias decided then, he was going to use every last one of them to sort out what had suddenly become his little family.

CHAPTER EIGHT

BETH WOKE TO the sight of a breakfast tray on the table by her bed and then, instantaneously, remembered what had happened last night and was gripped with panic.

There was no sign of Elias but then, beside the breakfast tray, she saw a note.

No change that I know of.
Thought I'd go over and see her.
Elias.

She felt better for knowing that he was there and she took out her phone and looked at the pictures of her baby.

There was little charge left on her phone and, seeing that, she decided to make a very difficult call before it went flat.

The phone rang a few times and she knew that she may have missed her parents. Her father would already be at the church but her mum sometimes headed over a bit later and she hoped that that was the case this Sunday.

It was.

'Mum, it's Beth. I don't have much charge on my phone so if it cuts out that's why.'

'What's wrong?'

Her mum, Beth knew, could tell from her voice that something was.

'I went into labour just on midnight…'

'But it's far too soon, what are they doing to stop it?' Jean asked, and Beth could hear her mother fighting not to panic.

'I had her at twelve thirty, a little girl…'

'Beth?'

'I haven't really seen her, Mum, she's on the neonatal intensive care unit. I'm waiting for my blood pressure to come up and then I can hopefully go over to see her and then I'll know more.'

'Well, I'll come now…'

'I'm in London,' Beth said, and the distance, not just physical, that had come between them since she'd broken the news of their pregnancy widened—once her parents had known her every move. 'I was here for Mr Costas's restaurant opening…'

'That's right.'

She saw her mother maybe once a month now. Jean would come over to Edinburgh with

little cardigans she had knitted and an enve-
lope with some money in it from her father.
The visits were terribly strained. They loved
her, they were just so very disappointed in her
and, yes, her father was ashamed too.

'I'll come as soon as I can,' Jean said. '*We'll*
come.'

Beth doubted that her father would. She simply could not see a happy reunion over an incubator. She knew her father and the hurt was
great. It might be years, if ever, before they
properly reconciled.

'I hate to think of you alone there,' Jean said.

Beth didn't correct her and say that she
wasn't alone and that Elias was here.

They weren't together, he wasn't even sure
that it was his baby, and so, Beth decided,
there was no point confusing her mother.

'Did you get to see her at all?' Jean asked,
and Beth looked up and saw that Elias was
standing in the doorway.

'I did,' Beth said, relishing the memory of
the moments she'd had with her child. 'I had
a little hold when she was born. She's got red
hair and she's a feisty little thing. Mum, my
phone's going to go flat soon. I'm at St Patrick's on the maternity ward, but once I've
charged my phone I'll send you the photos that

I have. You'll need to go and charge your mobile phone if you want to see them.'

Beth knew it would be sitting in her father's office drawer!

'I'll do that and then I'll go and look at train times. You'll call me back?'

'I shall.'

'Give her our love. I'll go and tell your dad now. He's over at the church.'

The phone cut out then and she looked up as Elias came in.

'How did they take it?'

Beth shrugged. She really didn't want to speak about her parents with him. 'Did you see her?'

Elias nodded. 'I think she looks a bit more rested. The nurses were handing over so I couldn't stay for long. She's got a nurse called Terri looking after her this morning. She seems very good and she says she's looking forward to you coming over as soon as you're able.'

He'd been very impressed with Terri. The baby had needed another IV line and Elias had stayed as the anaesthetist had inserted one into her scalp.

Terri had been unfazed when Elias had said that he'd prefer to stay and had worked calmly, explaining things every step of the way.

A midwife came in then to do Beth's observations.

'I want to go over to the NICU and see my daughter,' Beth told her.

'Your blood pressure is still very low.'

'Then I'll need a wheelchair.'

Elias gave an unseen smile because nothing was going to stop Beth.

First up, though, she had to freshen up and the midwife walked with her to the bathroom as Elias went and found a wheelchair.

Beth had a shower and glanced in the mirror at her wild red hair. She didn't even have a hair tie with her to try and hold it down.

She put on a fresh gown and a very welcome dressing gown and, given all that she had with her in the shoe department were stilettos, she was given a pair of plastic shoe covers to put on her feet.

Elias had found a wheelchair and it was he who wheeled her across once the midwife had rung over to NICU to tell them to expect her.

They didn't speak on the way.

He pressed the intercom and they were let in and told that she could go through now or someone could come down and speak with her first.

Beth chose to go straight through.

First, as instructed to, she carefully washed her hands and so did Elias.

They passed what looked like a glass-windowed storeroom full of empty cots and then to an area that seemed more like the control panel of a spaceship. To the left was an area, Beth would later find out, where the most intensive care was given.

And then a nurse smiled and waved her over and introduced herself as Terri. Finally Beth got to see her little girl.

She was lying flat on her stomach—Beth thought babies curled up and told the nurse the same.

'She hasn't much muscle tone,' Terri explained. 'They can get themselves into some pretty amazing positions.'

Terri was going to be Baby Foster's primary nurse, she told Beth. 'So, while she's this tiny, whenever I'm on duty, I'll be looking after her. I'll get to know her little ways. Not as well as you, of course, but I can be another voice for her.'

That helped.

'Can I hold her?'

'Not just yet,' Terri said. 'I know you're desperate to but she's very tired and we're trying to keep her rested and not over-stimulated.'

'I thought they liked to be held.'

'They do,' Terri said, 'but moving her will be a stress for her at the moment.'

Instead, she showed Beth how to touch her baby but it didn't feel enough.

'Do you have a name for her?' Terri asked.

Beth shook her head. 'I thought I was having a boy.'

Instead, she had a girl and one so tiny and delicate that it was scary.

They spoke about Beth's milk and how someone would come and see her back on the maternity ward to discuss accommodation, but it all went over her head. All she could see was her little girl.

An alarm sounded loudly and Beth jumped but Terri remained calm and started flicking at the baby's feet.

'I'm just reminding her to breathe,' Terri said soothingly, but it completely terrified Beth.

Even Elias, who had seen such things before, found he was holding his own breath and gripping the wheelchair very tightly as not only their baby's breathing but also her heart rate dropped.

Terri rubbed the tiny back and arms and finally the baby took a breath. Elias saw the look of terror in Beth's eyes.

'Has she done that before?' Beth asked.

'She has,' Terri said. 'It happens with babies that are premature.'

And Terri went through everything again— how she would have trouble regulating her breathing and temperature and feeding for now, but it was different hearing it to witnessing it.

It was exhausting.

After half an hour Beth nodded when Terri suggested that she go back to the maternity ward for a rest.

Elias took her there and wearily she climbed into bed.

'I should feel better for seeing her but I don't.' She admitted to Elias what she could barely admit to herself. 'It doesn't feel like she's mine.'

'I was the same,' Elias told her. 'She had that hat on and I didn't really recognise her at first but then when she opened her eyes I felt a lot better. You didn't get that today but it will happen soon.'

Beth nodded and looked over as a midwife came in.

She was hoping that it might be to draw the curtains so she could get some sleep, but she had yet to learn that she had entered a world where sleep was a rare luxury.

Instead, it was time to attempt to expel some colostrum, she was told.

'You can go,' she said to Elias, but then Beth remembered something. 'I haven't checked out of the hotel.'

'I can do that,' Elias offered. 'Is there anything else you need?'

She handed him a list that the midwife had given her as well as another list she had been given on NICU.

'I need everything on it!'

'Okay.'

'And I need my phone charger.'

It felt so strange to have Elias back in her life and yet there was no time to think about things. After he had gone she was too busy trying to get some precious drops of colostrum for her daughter to have.

Then the doctor came down from NICU and spoke with her at length, and after that Beth was visited by the social worker.

Because the baby was so premature and because she was so far from home, she would have a room next to the NICU unit.

'There's a shared kitchen and lounge area and the bathrooms are shared, but you and Elias can both stay...' She checked her notes. 'No other children?'

'No.'

'I have to check because if either of you have other children from a previous relationship, sadly they can't come into the parents' area. It gets too noisy and we've had problems with parents going off to check on their baby and leaving a toddler.'

'No.' Beth shook her head and then added it to the mental list of things she had to find out about Elias.

'So, when you're discharged tomorrow, head up to NICU and Rowena, the accommodation co-ordinator, will show you your room.'

And, in between all of that, there were texts from Elias.

What's the hotel's room number?

She had only given him the swipe card from her purse.

1024

He found it.

She really hadn't packed much.

There was an overnight bag and he filled it with the few things that were in the room and closed the door.

Then he opened the door again and retrieved

her phone charger. He did another quick sweep of the room and found a notebook.

He put it in the bag and then checked out.

And he took himself shopping and sent another text.

I need your clothes size and bra size.

She replied.

And later, as he stood a touch bemused in the 'feminine products' aisle, he had another question.

With wings or without?

Talk about get to know each other, Beth thought.

With. Could you get me some hair serum?

Then she felt guilty for worrying about things like hair serum when her baby was so ill.

Elias read her texts and looked at the lists and then gave up pretending he knew what he was doing. He headed to a very large, exclusive, famous store. There he spoke with a very helpful woman who asked about Beth's colouring.

Having handed over the lists, Elias went down to the baby department.

He knew that his little girl wouldn't be wearing clothes for ages but he bought an outfit for premature babies.

Even their smallest would be too big.

And maybe it was a lack of sleep, or just the shock of it all, because it suddenly hit him and Elias found himself standing in a baby department and on the edge of tears.

'Don't lose it now,' he told himself.

The last thing Beth needed was a blubbering mess yet he was suddenly a father and, even more surprisingly to Elias, he was in love with someone just a little bit bigger than his hand and terrified he was about to lose her.

Then he thought of Beth—she was simply a click away from finding out who he was and reading about his salacious past.

Not just the fatherhood accusations but the rather debauched playboy lifestyle he had lived for a while.

He knuckled his eyes and dragged in a deep breath and fought for calm. When he opened his eyes, it was to see a little pink bear, sitting on a glass shelf, wearing a little crown.

His Princess.

Elias bought it, along with a couple of pieces of clothing and a small cream blanket.

Terri had suggested that he get one that Beth would wear against her chest for a few hours. It would go in the incubator when it was time for the baby to be fed.

The baby.

She needed a name.

Having collected the purchases, Elias drove back to the hospital and as he did he took a phone call from his mother.

'I just wanted to discuss your birthday,' Margarita said. 'I thought after lunch we could schedule an appearance on the balcony...'

He sat at the traffic lights and caught sight of himself in the rear-view mirror and tried to imagine her reaction if he told her that he was, as of a few hours ago, a father.

The palace PR machine would move swiftly. Alvera would be dispatched to deal with Beth and Elias would be told to step back.

He knew how they worked, he'd been at the end of it on several occasions. He could well remember the icy treatment the woman received who had accused him of fathering his child.

Elias didn't want that for Beth.

The light turned green as his mother awaited his response. They never bothered with small talk.

'I'm working over my birthday. In fact, I'm

going to be staying in London for the next couple of months at least,' Elias told her. 'Don't go making any plans on my behalf.'

'You have to come back. It's your thirtieth!'

'I won't be there.'

'Elias…'

'No.' It was as simple as that now. There was no way he would be leaving his daughter for his thirtieth birthday, of all things.

It was *her* birthday today.

'I have to go, I've got another call coming in.'

He simply rang off.

Elias had no idea where he and Beth were headed—after all, they had been together for only one night.

He just knew he wasn't going to subject her to the demands of his family at such a fragile time.

And just as he was getting a grip on things, just as he was starting to think he knew something of the world he had entered, Beth's voice came on the line and filled the car.

'Elias!'

He went cold when he heard her distress.

'You need to get here. She stopped breathing…'

CHAPTER NINE

IT WAS THE scariest thing she had ever seen.

After lunch, feeling better for a sleep, Beth went back up to spend some time with her daughter, and this time she walked over to the NICU.

Chloe, the ward assistant, waited while she washed her hands and then took her through. The baby was still asleep on her stomach and her arms were up by her head. Terri patiently explained things again.

'There are things that we need to do for her until she is able to,' Terri said. 'At this stage they can't regulate their own temperature and they don't quite have the sucking reflex, and they get very tired, so we put a tube down and give her your milk.'

Beth nodded.

It was a very tiny amount she had managed, with the midwife's help, to express, but Terri said it was a fantastic amount and to keep going with it.

'And they forget to breathe,' Terri said, 'so we have to remind them.'

'Doesn't the machine breathe for her?' Beth asked. It was all incredibly confusing.

'This isn't a ventilator,' Terri explained, 'it's called CPAP.' She had already told Beth this but her brain felt like cotton wool at the moment.

Then Beth startled as a machine alarm went off and Terri gave the baby a little rub to nudge her to breathe, as she had done when Beth had visited before.

Except this time she didn't breathe.

Terri rubbed her little feet and Beth watched in silent panic as her baby's heart rate slowed down and another alarm sounded.

'What's happening?' she asked.

'Remember I told you about the As and Bs?' Terri said. Yes, she had told Beth about apnoea and bradycardia, that when they didn't breathe their heart rate could slow down.

Terri opened up the incubator and turned the tiny baby onto her back.

Her colour was changing and another nurse came over and set up a little bag and mask to breathe for her. Beth was starting to lose it.

'Come on.' Chloe, the ward assistant, was

helping her out of the main area as the neonatologist made his way over.

She looked back and there were quite a few people around the incubator and it was even more frightening than when she had been born.

'She's going blue…'

'Just wait here,' Chloe told her. 'Someone will come in and speak with you just as soon as they can.'

She was just left there.

Standing.

A woman was making coffee and stopped what she was doing when she saw Beth's anguished face.

'What's happening?' she asked as Beth stood there. 'I'm Shelly. I've got a little one in there…'

She was another mum, Beth realised, and at the same time it dawned on Beth that she herself really was a mum.

'I need to call her father…' Beth was in utter panic as she tried to turn on her phone but realised it was dead.

'Here,' Shelly said, and looked in her bag. She handed over a portable charger, which Beth plugged into her phone.

She called Elias and then Shelly handed her a mug of coffee.

It tasted too sweet because Beth didn't take sugar but also good, and she looked at Shelly and told her what was going on.

'She stopped breathing and her heart slowed down…'

'It happens,' Shelly said, but not blithely. 'My little boy was born at twenty-five weeks, he's been here for twelve weeks now.'

'Twelve weeks?'

'Yes.' Shelly nodded. 'They know what they're doing in there. It's the scariest thing to see but it happens. My little one can go home when he's managed five days without a run of apnoea…' She stopped talking for a second and looked up and saw a slightly breathless Elias. 'Is this Dad?'

It was.

'I'm Shelly.'

He nodded to Shelly as he sat down and Beth told him all that had happened.

In the midst of it, another couple were led in by Chloe. Elias recognised them as Amanda and Dan, the parents of the twins who had been admitted last night.

'Hi,' Elias said, but his greeting wasn't returned.

They had just been sent out to wait too, he realised as Amanda took out her phone to make a call.

'Why won't someone come and talk to us?' Beth shivered.

Because, Elias guessed, they were hellishly busy, but he stood up. 'I'll try and see what's going on.'

'They won't let you—' Beth started, but Elias had already gone.

He went to the unit and nodded to Chloe, asking if he could go through, but she said that she'd need to check.

'Sure.'

Elias knew it was imperative that he stay calm so he took time washing his hands and finally Chloe returned.

'Terri says you can come through but you need to stay back.'

'I know.'

Terri glanced up as he came over. There was another nurse with her as well as the neonatologist, Vince. 'It's going to be a while until Vince can come and speak with you.' She nodded in the direction of another incubator where there was more frantic work going on.

He knew it was one of the twins.

'That's why I came in to see what was happening.' Elias nodded. 'I shan't get in the way.'

'Good man.'

Vince was writing up her chart and gave a brief nod to Elias but he was now being called over to the other incubator where a large group had gathered.

'She's doing better,' Terri explained. 'But it would have been very scary for Beth. Her heart rate dropped down to fifty and we had to bag her. She's had a few runs of bradycardia but this one was quite extensive and Vince has decided to start her on a caffeine infusion. She's having a bolus dose now.'

Last night, during the delivery and afterwards, he had done all he could to keep his emotions in check and he was doing that again now. Elias knew they were bending the rules, letting him in, and if he gave in to the panic that was building he would be promptly shown out.

He watched the nurses work on her and every now and then Vince or another doctor came back and checked in.

They were seriously stretched, Elias could see, yet there was an air of focussed calm around the incubator.

She was starting to move her little arms and Terri explained that the infusion might make her jittery.

'You can bring Beth back in when you think she's ready,' Terri said to him. 'Don't rush it, though.'

'I shan't.'

He headed back out to the waiting room and looked at Beth's pale face. He ached for all she had been through alone.

She wasn't alone now.

Dan was pacing and Shelly was sitting with her arm round Amanda—it really was a heartbreaking room.

'She's okay,' Elias said. 'They've started her on a caffeine infusion…'

'Caffeine?'

'It's a stimulant,' Elias explained. 'She's having a loading dose now and then she'll stay on it for quite some time.'

'Can I see her?'

'In a little while,' Elias said, and took Terri's advice not to rush in. 'Beth, this sort of thing is going to happen.'

'I know, they warned me, but—'

'It's normal here,' he gently explained. 'She's going to need a lot of support.'

And so was Beth, he knew.

'I need to get a portable phone charger,' she said, and Elias nodded and watched as she struggled to stay in control. 'I had to borrow one.'

The neonatologist came to the doorway and Beth gripped Elias's hand, but Elias realised with a sinking feeling that he hadn't come to speak with them.

'Amanda and Dan,' Vince said. 'Come on through to my office and I'll speak with you there. Bring your drinks with you.'

Elias glanced at Shelly as they walked off and saw her expression was grim.

'Come on,' Elias said to Beth. 'Let's go and see her.'

And when they did, all the trouble she had just caused was instantly forgiven—she was on her back, her eyes open, and her little legs and arms were moving.

'She likes her caffeine!' Terri smiled.

'Hello there, little one,' Beth said, doing her best to keep her voice positive and calm. She smiled as her daughter turned to the sound of her voice.

The little hat was off. Beth could see the tufts of red hair and she recognised her baby again.

And then Elias remembered that he'd bought a present. He went back to the car and took out Beth's shopping, which had been neatly packed in a leather bag. He dropped it in her room but the little pink bear he brought up to the NICU.

It was nice that she had a toy.

'She needs a name,' Elias said. 'Have you thought of any?

'Not yet.' Beth had, in fact, chosen a name—

Eloise—but that had been when she'd thought she would never see Elias again.

Yet he was here now and she was glad of it.

Not just for her daughter's sake but for her own.

He was calm, he was patient and he didn't rush her as she struggled to adjust to this new world.

In the evening Elias went in search of dinner at the hospital canteen and returned with two burgers. They sat at the table in the parents' room on NICU.

'You should try and get some sleep, Beth,' he suggested.

'I don't want to leave her,' she admitted.

'I'll stay,' he offered.

'All night?' Beth checked, and he nodded.

She looked at him and could see the dark shadows under his eyes but she wasn't really in any state to feel sympathy or to realise that he hadn't slept at all last night.

Beth just felt better knowing that he would be here with their baby.

CHAPTER TEN

BETH WOKE AT four in the morning and she had two new friends sitting on her chest!

Her milk had started to come in.

The midwife arrived with a pump and though Beth was more tired than she had ever been, she remembered what Terri had said about a blanket with her scent on and wondered if Elias had remembered to get one.

She opened up the wardrobe and blinked because instead of a jumble of carrier bags there was a large, soft, leather holdall. She pulled it out and placed it on the bed.

Yes, there was a lovely little cashmere blanket and amazing toiletries too.

There was hair balm—and there was even nipple cream!

And the clothes were, well, extremely nice.

The sort that a new mother in the colour supplement of a Sunday paper might wear.

They were all colour co-ordinated and

folded and a peek at the label told Beth they were also expensive.

It unsettled her. She didn't know exactly why, just that it did.

She couldn't get back to sleep so she watched a few infomercials on the television and finally the news came on.

The world was happily carrying on, of course.

She had some tea and toast and was just about to have a shower and head up to NICU when her phone rang.

'Hi, Mum,' Beth said.

'I'm sorry to ring so early but I'm just going in to Edinburgh to get the train. How is she?'

And Beth honestly didn't know what to say. She didn't want to scare her mum and yet she knew she had to prepare her for all that was to come.

'She's up and down,' Beth told her. 'I'll talk to you both once you've seen her.'

'It's just me coming, Beth,' Jean said. 'Your father's starting a cold. You know how he takes one every year.'

Beth closed her eyes in frustration. Their granddaughter was hanging on to life and her father refused to get on a train for a cold.

Tears were pouring down her cheeks as she thought of the last time she had seen her father, and as she wiped them with the back of her hand she looked over and saw Elias standing at the door.

'I should be there about one,' Jean said. 'I'll get the four p.m. train home.'

'I'll see you then,' Beth said, and ended the call. 'How is she?' Beth asked Elias.

'She's had a good night.'

Elias hadn't.

Every alarm had jerked him out of a slight doze, and there had been many, many alarms going off in the NICU.

After he had spoken to Beth he intended to go home and grab a couple of hours' sleep. He would ring around the various hospitals that he worked at and cancel the shifts that he had lined up.

At least, that was the loose plan.

He could see that Beth had been crying and rightly guessed that she had been speaking with her parents.

There was so much to put right and Elias just didn't know how.

'Did you get any sleep?' he asked.

'A bit,' Beth said, and then she sat up. Even she laughed when his eyes drifted to her two new friends.

'They woke me up at four.'

'I bet they did.' Elias smiled.

She was glad that he didn't ask who had been on the phone, she wasn't ready to discuss her parents with him, and she was also glad that when a little while later a midwife came to run through the paperwork for her discharge, he said that he was going to go to the canteen to get something to eat.

It was all pretty straightforward.

She was given a form that would need to be filled in to register the birth.

'That has to be done within six weeks,' the midwife explained. 'And you'll need to be seen for a postnatal check five to six weeks from now. I've made you an appointment here.'

'What if I'm back in Edinburgh? Do I ring…?' Beth asked, and then stopped herself. Yesterday she had been told that the baby would likely be here for eight weeks at least. The only reason she might be back in Edinburgh was if her baby didn't make it. 'Actually…'

'It's okay, Beth.' The midwife understood the sudden tears in her eyes. 'If for any reason you can't make it a call would be appreciated and we'll arrange a referral for you.'

Beth nodded.

'For now it's on the fourteenth of February. Valentine's Day.'

Beth rolled her eyes.

And then she rolled them again when the midwife spoke about contraception.

'I know it's absolutely the last thing on your mind right now, but please, Beth, don't be a woman already pregnant at her postnatal check, unless of course you want to be.'

'Oh, no!'

'Intercourse can be resumed whenever you feel ready to but don't rely on breastfeeding as contraception.'

'I shan't.'

'You can start on the mini-pill. We recommend that three weeks after giving birth.' She handed her the shiny foil packets.

They'd be going straight to the bottom of her toiletries bag, Beth decided, but she took them anyway.

And once she was dressed she could leave.

It felt too soon.

Beth put a load of hair serum through her wild locks and then tied them back. She dressed in very nice yoga pants, soft shoes and a button-up top, and if she hadn't had a wobbly stomach she might have looked as if she was going out for a jog.

Elias was sitting in the chair when she came out of the small bathroom.

'I've been yummy mummy-fied,' Beth said.

'Meaning?'

'Nothing.'

She was disconcerted, that was all. Being dressed in his expensive choice of clothes for her felt a little like being dressed in clothes her parents deemed suitable. When she'd moved to Edinburgh, Beth had left most of her wardrobe behind and had had fun finding out for herself the clothes she liked. Oh, what she was wearing was the least of her troubles today, but it felt further proof that there was nothing familiar in her world any more.

They headed over to the NICU and though they were buzzed through, Beth frowned when she was told that she couldn't go onto the unit.

'The ward round is about to start,' Chloe explained. 'It's to do with patient confidentiality. You can only come through in exceptional circumstances.'

'I see,' Beth said, even if she didn't.

She found herself leaning against Elias.

His arm was around hers and it was just a matter of holding each other up as Chloe explained things to the newbies.

'They normally last for an hour except on Mondays and Fridays when they tend to run a lot longer. Rowena, the Accommodation Co-ordinator, will take you over to the parents' wing. Just have a seat in the parents' room and I'll let her know that you're here.'

Beth sat there and, no, she did not understand why she could not see her baby because there was a ward round.

'Patient confidentiality!' Beth rolled tired eyes. 'It's not like the babies can talk...' But then her voice trailed off. Amanda and Dan had arrived and were let in to see their babies and suddenly Beth felt very shallow—she never wanted exceptional circumstances to apply to them.

'I shouldn't have joked.'

'Beth...'

They didn't really know each other, yet the little barb about talking babies had made him smile. He was new to this too, unsure what hat he had on, doctor hat or new-dad hat.

'We're just finding our way,' he told her.

'I've never been in hospital before. Even my antenatal checks were held in an annexe attached to the hospital. It's like a foreign language.'

'I know,' Elias said.

He did.

Even with his profession and experience, it was totally alien to him.

They were shown around the parents' wing.

The coffee room, the fridge and all the rules that went with it.

There was a laundry and a long list of instructions about how and when it could be used.

'We had a father bringing in the week's washing for his wife to do, so we have to be specific,' Rowena explained. 'And we don't have an iron for the same reason, as well as for safety concerns.'

Beth was just very glad to have somewhere so close to her baby.

They found themselves in a small bare room and it would seem that this was to be home for the foreseeable future.

There was a desk, a chair and a small double bed made up with starched hospital sheets and blankets. They fell onto it and lay side by side on their backs, looking up at the ceiling and still spinning because of all that had taken place.

'The last time I was lying down,' Elias said, 'she wasn't even born.'

'Were you asleep when I came in?' Beth asked, remembering how rumpled and unshaven he'd appeared.

'Yes,' Elias said. 'Mandy came and woke me up and said there was a premature baby about to be born.'

'When did you realise it was me?' Beth asked.

'As soon as I saw you.'

'You were very calm,' she said.

'Not on the inside.'

'It is what it is.' Beth recalled his words. 'My dad says that.'

'How did they react to the news of your pregnancy?'

She hadn't been ready to go there but she was now. 'I told Rory first.'

'Your ex?'

Beth nodded. 'He asked if we could get back together. I was about twelve weeks pregnant by then, so I told him.'

'So you told him you were pregnant?'

'Yes.' She nodded. 'He was terribly shocked, of course.'

'Shocked?' Elias checked. 'Did he think it was his?'

'No, no...'

'So why was he *terribly* shocked?'

It seemed an odd choice of words to him. Terribly concerned, perhaps, or even hurt or jealous, but shocked?

'Well, that I'd...' She shrugged. 'You know.'

He was really intrigued now and he looked at her but she didn't return his gaze. He looked at her little pointy nose and then down at her pinched lips and saw that she was trying not to smile.

'Did you take ages to agree to sleep with him?'

'Can we move on?' Beth said.

'No.' Elias smiled but then it faded when she admitted the truth.

'It took ages for him to agree to sleep with me. I think he lost a lot of respect for me when he found out what I'd done.'

'We did nothing wrong, Beth.'

Oh, there were things he might change if there was a magic wand handy but he refused to regret that night and, more than that, he refused to let her be ashamed of it.

'Rory knew how my parents would react. He actually offered to say that the baby was his.'

Elias didn't like that, not one bit. It just amplified how he might have had a daughter and never known.

'It was nice of him,' Beth said, 'but I didn't want to be back with him and—'

Elias interrupted her. 'Could I suggest it was a bit opportunistic rather than nice?'

He saw that she gave a slight smile at his perception.

Elias said all the wicked things she thought but never voiced.

She turned her face to him.

They stared into each other's eyes, as they had on the beach, but there was colour and history now.

'Did you consider it?' he asked, and she liked it that she felt able to answer him honestly.

'I did,' she said in her lovely soft accent. 'But, you see, Rory is quite slight and fair and I thought I might be having a boy and that at some point we'd have to explain the tall hairy Greek in the village…'

They shared a laugh, just a small one, and then his faded.

He wasn't Greek.

They really were two strangers yet somehow they had to work things out so he listened as she continued to speak.

'And I think, as nice as it was of him to offer, he'd have held it against me—"the time Elizabeth strayed…"' As she stared into his eyes, she explained, 'I'm Elizabeth when my parents are cross.'

'How were they when you told them?'

He watched her nervous swallow and saw that she struggled for a moment before answering.

'I was sixteen weeks by the time I got up the courage. They, of course, wanted to go for

Rory's blood but I then had to tell them that it wasn't his.'

And he stared back at her.

'That was the biggest shock, I think. They're not bad people, Elias, but they are very set in their ways. It would have been hard enough to accept I was pregnant by Rory. They asked who the father was and I said his name was Elias. I didn't even know your surname.'

Her cheeks burnt red now as she recalled their horror and shock.

'They asked how we'd met and I said that we'd got talking on the beach after Mr Costas's party.'

And it sounded so sordid rather than the beauty they knew they'd made.

'I think my father wanted me to say that some passing fisherman had taken advantage. I think,' she said slowly, 'that it was worse for my parents to know I...'

Had wanted it.

'I'm sorry you went through all that.'

'So am I,' Beth said. 'I suggested that I get a flat in Edinburgh and they agreed it might be better that I move out. I haven't been back home since. I had to start my business up again as I didn't have the contacts from my church. Only Mr Costas kept me on. I've got a couple of new clients now and I've started a website, though I have to admit things have been very tight financially.'

'You don't have to worry about money.'

'Oh, but I do. I'll be fine for now. My dad has been sending me a bit every month and the social worker told me that given I'm breast-feeding I can have vouchers for the canteen.'

And he knew it would be too much to tell her all of it but he could tell her a bit if it eased her mind.

'Money's one thing you don't have to worry about,' Elias said. 'I'm loaded.'

'Really?'

'Really.'

She smiled. 'I might have to take you for all you've got.'

'Go ahead.'

Still they stared and still they smiled.

'My mum should be here this afternoon.' She looked into his eyes and asked him for something, 'Can you not be here?'

He could be offended but he didn't want Beth worrying about him meeting the family just yet and he did not want her knowing about his.

They were so new, not even a couple, the thread that bound them very fragile, and all their energy had to be on their child.

'I'll make myself scarce.'

'Thank you.'

'Do you have any other children?' Beth suddenly asked.

'No.' He gave a small laugh.

'Only they asked when I was signing for the room and I didn't know. I mean, there's so much I don't know.' And she made herself ask him. 'Are you seeing anyone?'

He didn't smile now.

'No, but...'

How did he tell her that there was a bride waiting in the wings, that he was a prince and the pressure that would be soon thrust upon them?

And Beth saw his hesitation.

'There's something you're not telling me, isn't there?' she checked, and he nodded.

'There's a lot I'm not telling you, Beth,'

'Good! Because right now I've got enough going on. I just don't want to know.'

There was no room for anything more in her head. She didn't want to hear about ex-wives or pasts or perhaps that soon he would be moving back to Greece and that they'd need to discuss access.

She just wanted her baby to make it through today.

'I'm scared for her, Elias.'

'I know.'

'She's so small.'

'She's better than we thought. Thirty weeks, almost to the minute.'

And, yes, she'd been conceived around one a.m. on a Saturday night.

'Have you thought of a name for her?' Elias asked.

'Bonny?'

He frowned and tried to picture 'Princess' before it and shook his head.

'Molly?'

'Nope.'

And then she told him the name she'd really considered, should she have a girl. 'Eloise,' Beth said, and slowly she opened up to him. 'It's a bit like your name.'

'I like it.'

And there, in that moment, he knew he was right to do this.

To simply shut the world out and focus on them.

CHAPTER ELEVEN

BETH SAT IN the NICU and didn't know how to greet Amanda when she walked past on her way out.

She had heard from Shelly that Amanda and Dan had lost one of the twins this morning.

The little girl.

And yet they couldn't go under for they were in the fight for their son's life.

Elias had gone home to fetch some clothes and, as Beth had requested, not be around when her mother came to visit.

'I haven't told my mother about Elias,' she told Terri. 'It probably sounds odd…'

'Not odd at all.' Terri smiled. 'You see it all here.'

'I'll bet.'

'Don't worry, I won't mention him.'

And then she looked over and smiled because a very neat redheaded woman was walking towards them.

'Mum!' Beth jumped up and then she watched as her very stoic mother looked in at her granddaughter and tears filled her eyes.

'When you said she was small…'

Terri was lovely with Jean and explained, with the same patience she had with Beth, all the equipment and what to expect and to hope for in the coming weeks. It was a bit much and after a few minutes by the incubator Jean said she might go and get a drink.

'I'll come with you,' Beth said.

'No, no,' Jean said. 'You stay with her.'

'Your mum just needs a moment,' Terri told her.

Yet she was gone for more than twenty and, in the end, Beth headed off to find her.

And there Jean was.

Sitting with Amanda in the parents' room and talking with her.

She really was a minister's wife and knew how to help people in dark times. Sometimes that angered Beth, that her parents could be so open and kind with others, just not with her.

It didn't anger her today, though. Poor Amanda deserved every kindness.

'I was just checking you were okay,' Beth said when her mother looked up.

'Amanda and I were talking about her wee daughter.'

'Your mum's going to make me a hat for her,' Amanda said.

'And I'll make a matching one for the little boy.'

'I'd better get back to him,' Amanda said, and Beth watched as she gave her mother a hug and then left.

'I'm sorry,' Jean said to Beth. 'I didn't expect to be so upset when I saw her. All those machines...'

'It's fine.' Beth understood how upsetting it was.

It was actually nice to have her mum there. Jean did as promised and had soon knitted little hats for the twins and one for her granddaughter, and she had also brought a suitcase of clothes for Beth.

Beth had left most of her clothes behind when she'd moved to Edinburgh but now they were handed back to her. 'I couldn't find any of your old nightdresses,' Jean said, 'so I put in a couple of mine for you.'

Joy!

Still, they had a hug as she left and Jean promised to be back next Monday and before that if things changed.

'You'll let me know if there's anything more that you need,' Jean checked.

Beth assured her she would and as she

headed back to her little room she texted Elias that the coast was clear. As she passed the parents' room she saw Amanda in there, having a cry and holding the two little hats.

Beth knocked on the open door and went in.

Oh, she wasn't good at this type of thing. Her parents were but Beth had always been sent off when anyone had come by the manse and been upset. At the most Beth would bring in tea, put it down on the table and then quietly leave.

More was required here.

'I'm so sorry, Amanda.'

Beth knew there was little she could say so she leant over Amanda and gave her a hug.

'I just got a text from my hairdresser,' the other woman told her. 'I was supposed to be there now, getting my hair done.'

'I know.' Beth nodded as she rested against her. 'I just had a message from a client all upset because I hadn't sent her the menus for her wedding.'

Everything was carrying on as they were suspended in this frightening world and they clung to each other for a moment.

'Dan's going to go and get some dinner soon...'

'No need.'

Beth looked up at the sound of Elias's voice.

He was holding some foil boxes and whatever was in them smelt delicious.

'I got loads,' Elias said.

He too hadn't known how to help or what to say but when he had stopped at his favourite restaurant to buy dinner for himself and Beth he'd decided to get extra.

He had seen how the parents all banded together and remembered how kind Shelly had been yesterday.

Everybody was kind tonight.

They left Dan and Amanda alone in the parents' room to share dinner undisturbed. Some headed for the canteen, while Beth and Elias took their meal into their room.

'How were your parents?' he asked, as she ate the most delicious beef bourguignon and creamy mashed potato.

'Mum was great but my father didn't come,' she told him. 'He has a cold, apparently.'

'Then he was right not to come.'

Beth gave a tight shrug. 'If he couldn't visit her, then he could at least have come and seen me,' she said.

'And maybe given you a cold?' Elias checked.

'I don't get them,' she said. 'I'm like my mother, I'm never sick.'

'Maybe he didn't want to risk it.'

He took the smouldering anger and doused it, but there was still the black hiss of smoke as it died, which lingered. Elias lay on the bed while Beth went to unpack the case her mother had brought.

He glanced up as she took out a billowing nightdress and, as she slammed it back into the case, he wisely said nothing.

Then she pulled out a blouse and skirt and threw them back and closed the lid.

She had left that life behind.

'Come here,' he said, and he patted the space beside him, and Beth came to lie down.

'I can't see my father and me getting past this,' Beth admitted.

'You shall,' Elias said with more conviction than he felt.

Elias knew a little of the difficult man Donald Foster was.

He really did.

That trip to Scotland to see in the New Year hadn't been an idle one. He had gone to her village and had found the church.

His intention had been to ask the minister about his daughter's whereabouts.

By the end of the sermon he'd decided against it, wondering if it might cause trouble for Beth.

He hadn't known she was pregnant, of

course, but hearing Donald Foster deliver a stern sermon about promiscuity and the hurt it caused to many made more sense now.

'I'm sure that one day—'

'You don't know him,' Beth snapped. 'You have no idea what he's like.'

'I've heard him deliver a sermon.'

She frowned.

'I came back to try and see if we could...' He gave a shrug, an awkward one. 'But I have to say, when he shook my hand at the end of the service I didn't think he'd take too kindly me asking the whereabouts of his daughter.'

'He wouldn't have,' Beth said, and she laughed a little at the thought of it, but then she was serious. 'You tried to find me?'

He nodded.

'Why?'

'You know why,' Elias said, and she frowned as she looked at him.

'I don't.'

'I missed you,' he said.

He had never missed anyone more than he had missed her.

His life had been spent guarding his emotions but that night he had let his guard down and it was lowering again now.

'I'm a bit crazy about you, Beth.'

It was a lovely surprise.

After so many horrible ones, the fact that he had come looking for her, and that they were now staring into each other's eyes and remembering that night, was for Beth the nicest surprise.

And then he kissed her, or rather they kissed.

They didn't roll into each other. Their mouths met and they shared a sweet, warm kiss that was needed tonight.

It was a moment when they tipped into being themselves rather than the terrified novice parents they were.

A tiny reprieve that their mouths afforded each other.

'We'll work it all out,' Elias said.

She believed then that they might.

CHAPTER TWELVE

HAVING A BABY in the NICU was the most intense experience of either of their lives.

Those first weeks were simply about her.

Eloise Foster.

Beth's two friends, who had arrived so spectacularly, very quickly decided they didn't want to be friends with Beth any more and started to disappear. By the time Eloise was ten days old Beth had to give up on the hope of being able to breastfeed her.

Yes, she'd got some colostrum but she felt as if her body had failed Eloise in so many ways and she was teary and tense.

Donald's cold went to his chest, which meant that by the time Eloise was two weeks old he still hadn't seen her.

Jean visited with a bag of hats that would keep half of the NICUs in London in supply.

Sometimes, just as they drew breath, they would find out that Eloise had a spike in temperature or that her apnoea was worse and her caffeine was being increased.

But there were good times too.

The second Monday of Eloise's life, when it was time for the big ward round and so time to leave the NICU, as Beth walked into their little room, Elias was pulling on a jacket.

'Come on,' he said, and handed her the coat she had been holding when she had come out of Mr Costas's restaurant.

'Where?'

'We're going for a walk,' Elias said.

Beth held her coat as they walked to the exit but feeling the gust of cold air from the door she put it on.

Kensington Gardens was just a short walk away and Elias stopped at a café and bought coffee and pastries as Beth went through her pockets.

There was her train ticket and a packet of mints and also a little note reminding herself to send Gemma the menu selections for her wedding in June. There was another little note with a couple of restaurant suggestions for another client who Beth had secretly nicknamed The Laziest Man Alive.

It felt as if she were looking at notes from another world, yet it was a world that was pulling her back to join in.

She wasn't ready, though, she thought as Elias came out and they walked over to the gardens.

It was grey and cold but it was good to be outside.

'I like coming here,' Elias told her.

'I've never been.'

They went to the Round Pond and sat watching the swans and just enjoying the cold.

'It's nice to get some fresh air,' Beth admitted. It was always so warm up on the NICU and feeling the cool damp breeze was refreshing. 'I ought to make a few phone calls this afternoon, sort out some of my clients.'

'Do you have many?'

'No,' Beth said. 'Mr Costas was the big one and I have a couple of small events that I guess I could pass over to my friend Jess, but I don't really want to lose the few clients I have.' She let out a sigh. 'I haven't got the headspace to do what I have to.'

'Like what?'

'I've got an anniversary luncheon to book and some guy who wants me to plan the perfect proposal.' She rolled her eyes. 'Men are so lazy.'

'Thanks.'

'Not you.' Beth smiled. 'He just hasn't got a

clue. I have to tell him everything. I'm charging him for it, mind.'

'What else?'

'I've a big wedding in June.'

'It's a long way off.'

'Not for this bride,' Beth sighed. 'She wants regular updates. I've told her what's happened and she's fine for now but she won't be for long. I was hoping this wedding would lead to more work, though.' She let out a tense breath. 'And please don't tell me I don't have to worry about money...'

'I wasn't going to.' Elias knew better than most that work wasn't just about money. His parents didn't understand why he chose to work weekends and nights when there was no financial need. 'This is your career.'

'And it's already taken a big hit,' Beth said. 'I used to get a lot of traffic from Dad. I knew everyone in the village and they knew me. It's different in Edinburgh.'

'What do you have to do?'

'Loads,' Beth said. 'There are all the contracts to sort and I need to draw up a list of flowers. She didn't like my suggestions.'

'Which were?'

'Well, it's a June wedding so the gardenias will be in. I thought she could have them on the pews with some tartan but...' Beth shrugged. 'I need to step back from my vision sometimes. She wants orchids and I have to source—'

'This week,' Elias interrupted, and was more specific. 'What do you *have* to do?'

'Oh. I've got to register her birth! They keep telling me…'

'That can wait,' Elias said, and not just to save himself. He knew how jumbled her mind was, given all that was going on. 'What has to be done for work?'

It was hard to turn her mind to work but maybe being away from the hospital and the soothing sight of the birds on the water helped.

'I've got to do the numbers for a luncheon in February. For the wedding I have to check her meal selections and then send the contracts for the venue for her to sign…' Beth shook her head. 'Maybe I'm taking too much on, I was already worried about getting a babysitter.'

'Well, that's already sorted.'

She turned from watching the lake to him.

'Beth, whatever happens between us, I'm going to be around for Eloise.'

He said it so calmly and without qualification that for the first time Beth glimpsed a future where Eloise had two parents.

Oh, he'd been great in the hospital—but now, outside the walls of it, they were sitting there, two adults discussing work and their child, and she felt the immense pressure loosen a touch.

'Why don't I get a printer?' Elias suggested.

'A printer?'

'You can sort out the contracts tonight. Tell your client that she'll have them this week. We can sort out the lazy guy's perfect proposal between us…'

'I can't do the luncheon.'

'Then pass that one on, but the rest you can manage. I could even go to the post office for you!' He was teasing her a little and it made her smile. 'You can do this.'

He stood and so too did Beth and they walked back to the hospital. She felt better for the small reprieve.

Better not just for the fresh air but for the conversation and the tiny return to a world that had been left on hold.

And there was a reward waiting for her when she arrived back on NICU—Terri asked if she would like to hold Eloise.

Finally.

She sat in a large reclining chair and opened up her top as told, and it took two nurses to sort out all the equipment but finally her baby was back on her chest as she had been the night she'd been born.

It was bliss, for both of them.

Eloise now had more muscle tone and she curled into a little ball on Beth's chest. It was magical to hold her. Beth kissed her little head and inhaled the sweet baby scent of her and it lasted an hour.

Holding her didn't happen every day but every day Beth was able to do something for Eloise, from changing her tiny nappy to giving her a massage, or just talking to her when she was awake.

And, *every* day, she and Elias went for a walk.

He carved out that time for them.

'Come on,' he would say, whatever the weather. Rain, a little bit of snow, even on such a windy day that it would have been more sensible to stay inside, they headed out.

That daily break was the most sensible thing they did.

They found out about each other and caught up on their own lives. Elias was being asked to work some shifts and, with the help of the printer he had bought for her, Beth was almost keeping up with things.

'It's freezing,' Elias said one morning as he looked at her pale lips. They had walked further than usual and were at the bandstand. The grass was icy and crunched beneath their feet but it was nice to walk and talk.

'We can head back if you want,' he offered.

'This isn't cold.' Beth smiled as she pushed her hands into her coat pockets. 'You should see winter where I'm from…'

'I have,' Elias said, and she smiled.

It was still hard to accept that he'd been in Dunroath, looking for her, and it meant a lot that he had.

She wished he'd asked her father about her. Yes, it would have been awkward and difficult, but it hurt that he hadn't.

She didn't say anything. Beth always held a lot inside.

'How cold does it get in Greece?' she asked instead.

'I'm not from Greece…' Elias told her as they walked. There was a little robin sitting on the bandstand, singing, and slowly they were revealing themselves to each other. 'I'm from a country called Medrindos.'

'Oh!'

'And it doesn't get that cold there. The winters are, I guess, like your spring.'

'Are you going to tell your parents?' Beth asked him.

'When I'm ready to.'

'Are you…' she made herself finish '…embarrassed?'

He gave a low laugh. 'No.'

'Ashamed.'

'Of you?' He laughed again. 'Never. Are you ashamed of what happened?'

She didn't know how to answer. That night had been the most amazing night of her life, and from that night she had a daughter she loved more than she'd thought possible…

'I just wish I hadn't hurt my parents so much.'

'They care,' Elias said. 'And when they see you're doing okay, which you are, they'll feel better.'

Beth doubted it.

'They will,' Elias said.

'Why haven't you told your parents,' Beth asked, 'if you're not embarrassed?'

'Because they tend to take over,' Elias said. 'And I want some time for us.'

'So do I,' Beth agreed. 'What are they like?'

Elias thought before he answered. 'I had a very privileged upbringing,' he told her, trying to slowly drip-feed in his past so that it would not come as too much of a shock. 'But I didn't see much of my parents.'

'What do you mean?'

'Well, my mother might put in an appearance at bedtime but we had nannies...'

'Nannies?' Beth said, frowning at the plural and assuming his parents had gone through staff quickly.

The truth, though, was worse.

'One each for my brother and me and a relief one for holidays and things. I don't want that for Eloise. I want her to know her parents.'

'She will.'

Beth couldn't fathom it. Oh, sometimes she felt stifled but her parents had been there for her every step of the way growing up, and they shared every meal.

'I want to be hands-on, Beth.'

'You already are. When you say they take over?' Beth asked, because she didn't understand. From the way he'd described them it sounded as if they were distant, yet he was concerned that they might interfere.

'Last year a woman said that she was pregnant with my child.' Elias turned when he saw that Beth had slowed down. 'My family got their lawyers involved and—'

'Was it your child?' Beth asked.

'No,' Elias said. 'We hadn't even slept together.'

'Then why would she...?' Beth quickly backtracked. 'It doesn't matter.'

'You can ask me,' Elias said, but Beth shook her head.

She wasn't ready to hear it all.

'I keep forgetting things,' Beth told Amanda one morning as they sat in the parents' room. There was a ward round on and Elias had gone to get some decent coffee.

'And me,' Amanda said. 'And I keep repeating myself! Dan keeps saying, "You've already told me that!"'

'And Elias.' Beth laughed, glad that she wasn't the only one losing her mind. She looked up when Rowena, the Accommodation Co-ordinator, put her head around the door.

'Beth, could I have a word?'

'Sure.'

Beth got up and walked with her to a small office.

'I know you're far from home but now that Eloise is improving and you're no longer breastfeeding we might need to look at alternative accommodation. We're okay for now, we've still got two rooms vacant, but we do need to prioritise the sickest babies and the feeding mums.'

'Of course,' Beth said.

'We're not kicking you out, we do have a few alternatives, depending on your budget…'

There was a house nearby that took in temporary boarders and there was also a small hotel, she was told. 'You'd still be able to use the parents' lounge and amenities,' Rowena explained.

And it was good news, Beth told herself. After all, it meant that Eloise was doing so much better.

She just couldn't imagine not being close to her.

As she walked back into the parents' room Elias was now there and chatting with Amanda.

'So are you doing anything to celebrate?' Amanda was asking him.

'No need.' Elias shook his head.

'Celebrate what?' Beth asked, smothering a yawn.

'His birthday.' Amanda smiled as she rinsed her cup. 'Did you forget?' she teased.

'I didn't know,' Beth said to him, once Amanda had left. 'How did she?'

'My brother just called.'

'Oh.'

He never really spoke about his family. Well, he'd tried to but Beth always blocked it.

When he'd told her that last year a woman had accused him of being the father to her unborn baby, she had clammed right up and told him they could do all that later.

And later was approaching now.

He wanted to talk to her, Beth knew.

There was so much to say and she was scared to hear it. While she knew they had to sort themselves out, they were still very new and fragile.

They were parents rather than a couple but that was starting to change.

Beth was beginning to come out of the fog, the daze of confusion she'd been wrapped in for the past three weeks.

'I've been asked to work this afternoon,' Elias told her. 'Someone's called in sick at short notice and they were so good when I had to leave that night.'

'Go,' Beth said.

'It's two till ten.'

'That's fine.'

The world was starting to trickle in, so much so that after she had held Eloise and had some precious time with her, she asked Terri if she could leave for a couple of hours.

'I thought you'd never ask.'

'You'll call if there's a problem?' Beth checked.

'Of course.'

Beth trusted Terri and, quite simply, she

needed to get out. She took the dress she'd been wearing when she'd gone into labour to the dry cleaner's and she even bought some clothes for herself.

Not a lot, but clothes that were more her own style. Leggings and tube skirts and a couple of wraparound cardigans that would be lovely to hold Eloise in, and then she went to buy a gift for Elias.

She had the photo of Eloise holding his finger, which had been taken on the day she was born, blown up a little and she chose a simple silver frame.

She bought a cake and when she was back in the parents' wing she wrote her name on the box and put it in the fridge.

Tonight they would talk, she decided.

She changed into her new clothes—a short skirt, thick tights and a black wraparound cardigan—and, feeling more herself than she had in a long while, she went back in to be with Eloise.

'Wow!' The nurse smiled when she saw her. 'It looks like getting you out did some good.'

It had done.

Wow! Elias thought with surprise as he walked through the unit and saw Beth standing over the incubator and talking with the nurse.

She turned and smiled when she saw him.

'Here's your dad,' Beth said to the baby.

Eloise was awake but sleepy and, Beth explained, needed her sheet changed as one of the IVs had leaked.

Beth was so much more confident with all the equipment now, Elias thought. The nurse was getting the sheet ready for a quick change while Beth would lift Eloise and sneak in a little extra hold. But, knowing he had missed out today, she stepped back.

Elias lifted the baby and held her for a moment as the sheet was changed and Beth watched.

He was so gentle with Eloise. He held her against him and looked down at his daughter as the incubator was prepared and the little pink bear put back.

'She's nearly asleep,' Elias said.

'Have a few minutes,' the nurse responded. Eloise was maintaining her temperature and heart rate well and was looking very content in her father's arms. When the large chair was brought over, he took a seat.

It was his first real hold of her and perhaps the best birthday present he could have had.

It wasn't long, but a lovely treat, and Eloise looked as if she was enjoying it as much as her dad. She stared up at him with sleepy eyes but soon it was over and Beth watched as he tenderly put her back.

'How was work?' she asked as they looked down at her sleeping form.

'It felt odd to be back,' Elias admitted. 'They've asked if I can work in A and E here tomorrow night.'

'Do.' Beth nodded. 'Come on, I've got a surprise for you.'

Elias groaned. He loathed birthdays, he really did. They had always been stuffy formal affairs or, in later years, an excuse to get blind drunk and pull.

'Come on.'

They walked into their room and though tiny it now felt like home. There was the printer she'd used to keep somewhat up to date with work. The anniversary luncheon was going ahead with Jess's help and Beth had almost planned the Lazy Man's perfect proposal for him. Gemma, the June bride, had her contracts and the menu was sorted.

Now Elias sat on the bed and she walked in with a shop-made cake and a candle and the gift.

He looked at Eloise's tiny fingers wrapped around his, and recalled being so grateful that she could do even that.

'You know she's yours,' Beth said.

'I do.'

'We need to register her…'

'I know.' They'd managed three weeks and they were all the better for it. No, not a couple but certainly they were united parents.

And maybe nearly a couple too, Elias thought as he pulled her down onto his lap.

She looked again like the woman he had met that night.

Oh, she was in winter clothes but she was dressed like Beth rather than a woman who'd been dressed by a personal shopper.

'I need to talk to you,' Beth said. 'The accommodation officer spoke to me today. They might need the room soon for another mother. I've got a couple more days here but she's given me some suggestions…'

He shook his head as she told him what they were.

'You'll come back to mine.'

'I feel like I've landed on you…'

'You have,' Elias said. 'And that's fine. We're sorting it out.'

And they would.

Soon she would be home, away from the hospital, and they could speak properly about things.

Work out what the two of them wanted.

Though that was working itself out now.

Beth had rolled her eyes when the midwife had spoken about sex, and certainly then it would never have entered her head that in three weeks' time she would be sitting on his lap, staring into his eyes and moving in for a kiss.

They had kissed once since Eloise's birth, but it had been a kiss she had been unable to define, a mixture of fear, relief, or maybe just emotion.

This kiss was pure want and deeply sensual.

His hands were in her hair and then they went down to her bottom and he shifted her in his lap.

It was intimate and it tipped her from mother to woman.

It shocked her.

Nicely so.

That in the midst of everything they could find each other.

She was breathless as she pulled back, stunned at her body's easy response to him because it felt as though a flame was warming her inside.

'Happy birthday,' she said.

'It is.'

And tonight they both got into bed and kissed some more, long, lazy kisses with their legs entwined as they made up for too many months apart.

And Elias had decided.

'You're coming home to mine.'

CHAPTER THIRTEEN

THEY SAT BESIDE the Round Pond. She would miss this, Beth thought.

'I've got some more shifts at St Patrick's coming up,' Elias told her, but what he didn't tell her was that on Monday he had an interview at The Royal.

Beth looked out at the pond.

'My lazy client emailed again,' Beth said. 'He wanted more suggestions for where to propose. I said he should take her skiing while there was still time. Apparently he's a brilliant skier, so I suggested a romantic proposal in the snow but, no, he wants something more low-key.'

'Like what?'

'Well, I said to take her to a nice restaurant, find out her favourite meal. I charged him fifty pounds for that bit of advice.'

Elias laughed. 'And what did he say?'

'He doesn't know her favourite food. I tell you he's useless.'

'I thought you liked your job?'

'I do,' Beth said.

'Well, you're not very nice about your clients.'

'I'm not a doctor, I can have a laugh about them.'

'Well, I think you're being hard on him. I don't know your favourite meal,' he pointed out.

'We're not about to get engaged! Anyway, I'm easy. We had a French couple come and stay with us at the manse. A couple of times she insisted on cooking. I'd never even had garlic till then.'

'How old were you?'

'Fourteen. My parents like very plain food. Fantastic as it is, it's very plain.'

'So what did she make?'

'Cassoulet.'

'That's your favourite?'

'Oh, no, it was awful,' Beth said. 'I don't like beans and it was full of big fat ones. It was terrible but we had to finish to be polite. Then she insisted on cooking again and we were all dreading it, but she made Chicken Provençal. It was the best thing I'd ever tasted and it was the same for my dad. It was amazing. My mum still makes it but you can't get *herbes de Provence* in our village. Well, you can, but they don't have lavender in them, and my mum doesn't put wine in—she uses white wine vinegar—and she doesn't use shallots, just onions. The Scottish man's Chicken Provençal, my dad calls it, but not when my mum's around…'

She didn't know why he found that so funny.

'What?'

'You take a long time to get to the point.'

'I'm Scottish, we like to wander,' Beth said. 'So what's your favourite meal?'

'Curry.'

Beth screwed up her nose.

'There's a lot of seafood where I'm from and lamb, but when I was a med student I had my first curry, and I knew I could eat it every night.'

'Well, I shan't be suggesting that he takes her for a curry,' Beth said.

'What does he look like?'

'I've never met him, we just email. Do you know he even asked me for help choosing the ring? I asked what her star sign was and he doesn't even know that.'

'You're right,' Elias said. 'He is useless.'

Then they turned to each other and smiled as there was yet another thing he didn't know.

'I'm a Gemini, Elias. There are two of me.'

She didn't have to explain that there was the prim and proper Beth but there was another one that was rarely on show.

'I know,' Elias said. 'And I like getting to know both.'

He was the only person, Beth realised, who ever had.

Beth had accumulated rather a lot of stuff and by the following afternoon it was all packed into bags and she was cleaning out her little corner of the fridge as she chatted with Amanda.

'I am so tired of take-away and canteen food.' Amanda sighed. 'Your mum said she'd bring me something home-made. When's she coming in again?'

'Tomorrow.'

'What about your dad? I haven't seen him visit.'

'No, he had a cold and then a nasty chest infection,' Beth told her, but she didn't go into detail. Amanda had enough on her mind.

Her little son, even after three weeks, was still smaller and younger than Eloise had been when she'd been born and Amanda had also buried a daughter.

They had grown close and Beth would miss

their chats late into the night or early in the morning. She was very glad that her mother made a fuss of Amanda but it niggled that Jean was kinder to virtual strangers than she was to her daughter.

Dan and Amanda weren't married. In fact, Dan had only recently left his wife.

Her parents saved judgment for Beth!

'Do they know about Elias yet?' Amanda asked.

Beth turned and smiled. 'You don't miss a thing, do you?'

'Nope.' Amanda grinned. 'I just see he disappears whenever your mother visits and she said…' Amanda stopped.

'Go on,' Beth invited.

'Well, your mum said something about you being a single mum and I didn't get it. I mean, Elias is here all the time.'

It would be her mother's fourth visit tomorrow and Beth was tired of hiding things. As they left the hospital to travel to Elias's apartment Beth took the opportunity to tell him what she had decided.

'I'm going to tell Mum that you're in the picture tomorrow when she visits,' she said as they drove from the hospital.

'Do you want me to speak to her?'

'No.' Beth shook her head.

'I'm more than happy to.'

'I know.' Beth nodded. 'I just think it's better if I tell her myself and then she can relay it back to my dad. Maybe next week…'

She cringed at the thought of them meeting him but then she remembered that Elias had been to the church and must have seen what her father was like.

'It's going to be very awkward when you do meet him,' she told Elias.

'You're telling me!' He turned and gave her a smile that said not to worry.

But she did.

And then after only five minutes or so they were pulling into an impressive stucco building and Beth found that she had something else to worry about…

'Where are we?'

'Home,' Elias said.

It was *very* close to the hospital.

Beth frowned.

And her frown only deepened as she walked through the serviced foyer and they took an elevator up to his apartment.

She was no expert on London real estate but something this central in London and so exquisite surely couldn't be his?

She had been about to ask if it was, or if he rented, but talking about money was something her parents had taught her was inappropriate. Not only that, there was so much about him she didn't know and was afraid to ask, scared that the bubble they had lived in these past weeks was soon to burst.

'How long have you lived here?'

'Six months,' Elias answered.

He had thought it low-key when he'd bought it. A simple three-bedroomed apartment.

But Beth was looking up at the high ceilings and the gorgeous fireplace in the formal lounge and he could see that she was uncomfortable.

She walked to a large sash window and peered out, staring at the gardens they had walked through most days.

'When you said you were loaded…' She took a breath. 'I didn't mean what I said about taking you for all you've got.'

'Beth,' he interrupted, 'I understand that you were joking.'

His wealth didn't reassure her—in fact, it troubled her.

Deeply.

She looked at him—he was wearing black jeans and a black jumper, except he was wearing them extremely well.

There was an elegance to him that she

couldn't quite explain. She had seen it the night he had walked along the beach.

She was in her leggings and the coat she had worn the night she'd had Eloise, and he watched her arms fold across her chest as if in defence.

Yes, Elias knew then that he had been right not to blurt out his identity. Beth was a complex person and unlike some of the more shallow women he had been with he knew that his title would not please her one iota.

'Even if I was joking, I was wrong,' Beth said. 'It's actually the other way around—you could take me for everything I've got.'

And all she really had was Eloise.

He could clearly afford a cleaner, despite working hour after hour at the hospital. The place was immaculate.

No doubt he could afford a nanny too and though he had said he didn't want that life for Eloise, Beth was starting to glimpse his power. She thought of her bedsit in Edinburgh and her fledgling career and had the terrible feeling that with a click of his fingers it could all be gone.

'I wouldn't do that to you,' Elias said, but there was a huskiness to his voice. He knew Eloise was his, he knew all that entailed.

Beth could be paid off, discreetly dealt with

and put down as a mistake from his past. But that wasn't an option.

The other option was daunting.

If they were a couple, if this relationship went where he was hoping it might, Eloise would be a princess. Elias had done his best to pull back from that life but a baby would change many things.

Yes, it was daunting indeed.

'What happens if we don't work out, Elias, what happens if I don't jump to your tune?'

'Have I once asked you to jump to my tune?'

She stood there in his stunning apartment and thought of the lawyers he could afford versus the one in her village that she couldn't even afford to retain.

'No, but I've got a home waiting for her in Edinburgh, Elias.' Beth thought of the little crib she had bought and the baby bath and all she had struggled to provide. 'What if I want to take her there when she's discharged?'

Elias didn't answer straight away.

He had an interview coming up. He had pictured life here. Oh, there was an awful lot to discuss.

'I'm going to ring in and cancel work.' Elias could see that she was overwhelmed.

'Please, don't.' She wanted a night alone.

'If there's a problem with Eloise at least you'll be there.'

No, Beth thought as he headed into work, his wealth was not soothing.

It was a relief to have a night to herself away from the hospital. After Elias had gone, Beth was checking that her phone was on when suddenly it rang.

She answered it straight away and then had a quiet panic when she realised it was her father.

She hadn't spoken with him in months.

'How are you, Beth?' Donald asked.

'I'm doing well.'

'And how is Eloise?'

'She's improving every day,' Beth said. 'Well, some days are better than others but she's getting there.'

'Your mother isn't well,' Donald told her. 'It's just the cold that I had but she thought it best that she not visit tomorrow. I'm going to be coming down.'

Beth closed her eyes.

She knew better than to hope for some tender reunion over the incubator. Her father had been very hurt and angry at Beth and even all these months later it remained. She could hear the strain in his voice and her responses were equally stilted.

She hurt too.

Terribly so.

The one time she had strayed, the one time she had broken out of the mould, she had been cut loose.

Oh, they hadn't thrown her out on the street, but they had been relieved when she'd suggested that she leave.

The money from her father was his attempt at duty, Beth knew.

Yet it was understanding and love she had needed.

'I'll be there around one,' Donald said.

'I'll look forward to it.'

She was, in fact, dreading it.

Instead of moving into Elias's bed, Beth opted for one of the guest rooms.

It wasn't some puritanical streak that kept her from his bed, it was the simple fact she wasn't ready to be living with him, sleeping with him, further into him than she already was.

She unpacked her bags and she looked at the yummy-mummy clothes Elias had bought for her and she looked at the impressive furnishings—there was the problem.

She didn't fit that mould either.

With her things unpacked, Beth pushed open the door to a sumptuous bathroom and then ran a deep bath, filled with bubbles and oils. She found out what wallowing meant because she did just that.

And there, away from the hospital, when she thought she would be fretting about Eloise, instead she was fretting about her feelings for Elias.

Deep feelings.

In the months they had been apart she had, to survive, closed her heart to the memory of them, but it was open wide now.

She was crazy about him and he had told her he was a little bit crazy about her.

It felt as if she was falling in love backwards and she had never been more confused.

The months before Eloise had arrived had been hell yet the weeks since she had been born had been made bearable by him.

Yet they were drawn together by circumstances and it didn't feel a lot to build a future on.

He had come to her village to find her, though, Beth thought as she pulled herself out of the bath. It hurt that he hadn't cared enough then to speak to her dad and to find out where she was.

It was nice not to put everything back in her toiletry bag once she had brushed her teeth and combed her hair.

And it was bliss not to have to wrestle a damp body into clothes before she stepped out of the bathroom.

Instead, she rubbed in some moisturiser and took her pill, as she had been doing since they'd kissed, and she headed for bed.

She'd had weeks of starched hospital sheets. She also knew that Elias was at the hospital should something happen.

Nothing happened.

No news really was good news.

On his break Elias headed up to the NICU and there was Eloise, asleep on her stomach, and she had wriggled her way to the top corner of the incubator.

The CPAP had gone and she was on a little oxygen delivered through nasal prongs.

He went back again in the morning before heading for home.

Terri had just come on duty and gave him a smile. 'How was Accident and Emergency last night?'

'Busy,' Elias told her.

'I didn't realise that you were the doctor who delivered her…' Terri commented as she checked Eloise's equipment at the start of her shift. 'I was just going through the paperwork yesterday.' She glanced over. 'That must have been scary.'

Elias nodded. 'It was.'

The dots were starting to join up, Elias knew.

Word would soon get out.

Oh, not from Terri, but the press were always snooping and he was just a click away from being found out.

For nearly four weeks he had been able to shield Beth from the huge changes that were coming into her life but time was running out.

'Would you like to hold her, Elias?' Terri asked.

'I would.'

'Get your top off, then.' Terri grinned.

He took off the top half of his scrubs and sat in the chair. Eloise was on a lot less equipment now, so it meant only Terri was needed to sort out her tubing and bring her over to him.

It wasn't the first time he had held her, but it was the first time he had sat alone in the quiet of morning with his daughter.

Eloise relaxed to his voice too. Every night he told her a little story and this morning he did too—he could have sworn she smiled.

She was growing a little every day, becoming more of a person every day. She was nearly four weeks old, or thirty-four weeks gestation.

Still early but finally, *finally* he and Beth were off the terror treadmill and starting to be able to focus a little on themselves.

He and Beth needed to start from the beginning, Elias thought as he gazed at his daughter. They hadn't even been out on a date.

'We'll have to put that right,' he told Eloise.

They needed a night out where they could get to know each other in a more usual way.

'Let me take a photo,' Terri said, and she did.

A gorgeous photo that Beth awoke to.

She was surprised to see it was seven in the morning. It had been the first uninterrupted sleep she'd had in weeks.

Eloise had a good night.

There was a photo attached of Elias in NICU, holding their baby against his bare chest, and they both looked so happy and content.

Beth drifted off into a twilight zone, remembering the night they had met.

Sitting on a beach, hearing the laughter coming across the water and looking out to the yacht.

And then a man walking, or rather at first she could just make out it was a person walking along a pier and then onto the beach. Taking his time, a bottle of champagne in hand...

'Beth?'

She heard a knock on her door and then his voice as it opened.

'I brought some breakfast.'

'Come in.' Beth sat up and turned on the side light. 'How was work?'

'It went really well,' Elias said.

He looked exactly as if he had been up all night and was a man who had lived off little sleep for weeks. He was unshaven and there were dark shadows beneath his eyes and she was caught between her dream and the reality of him here.

There was something she had just remembered. Something in her dream that called for closer inspection but it was like chasing steam—it simply dispersed.

And then she remembered the photo he had sent to her.

'You got a nice cuddle.'

'An hour,' Elias said. 'I even gave her a little feed. She's a very good listener.'

'Only because she can't talk yet.' Beth smiled. 'So, what were you talking about?'

'You.'

'I know I was difficult last night...' It was hard to articulate. 'I've done it on my own for months, Elias. I always thought my parents would be there for me.' She looked at him and she was scared to let herself think. 'I was always good and yet the first sign of trouble I was out on my own. She's all I have.'

'No.' He shook his head. 'I'm in this, Beth, you're not on your own.'

'I wanted a level playing field,' Beth told him.

'You've got one.'

He could tell she didn't believe him.

They had to be the level playing field, Elias knew.

They had to sort out all the bumps and the obstacles so they were together and strong as they faced all that was to come.

'I'd better get up,' Beth said.

'What time is your mother getting there?'

'It's my father that's coming.'

'Why don't you let me speak to your father?'

'You didn't the last time you had a chance to!' Beth challenged. It hurt that he hadn't and she revealed it now. Oh, she understood why, her father was very intimidating, but even so.

He could hear anger in her voice and Elias put down his drink and put his hand on her bare shoulder.

'Let me be there today, Beth…'

'No.' She shook her head. 'It will make

things worse. I just want him to see Eloise. Whatever happens between us is separate. If we don't work out...'

'Why do you keep saying we're not going to work out when we haven't even given it a try?'

'I want to try,' Beth admitted. 'And I know that hiding in the guest room isn't helping things, but it isn't the sex that I'm worried about.'

'I understand that.'

It was her heart.

Beth looked into his lovely dark eyes and she was scared of future hurt.

It hadn't hurt enough when she had ended things with Rory. Losing Elias, though, had the potential for agony.

He'd changed her world, not just because of Eloise. He made each day better.

'I thought we should go out tonight. Properly,' Elias said.

'A date?'

'I'll book somewhere, somewhere we can talk about us. Somewhere that isn't the hospital or my home...'

'I'd like that,' Beth agreed.

It was time for them, she realised.

Time to see if there was more than a baby binding them together.

CHAPTER FOURTEEN

THERE WAS A flare of hope as she stepped out onto the street.

It was like a flame burning in her chest that made the cold morning seem less so.

It was after nine and, knowing there was a big ward round this morning, and it might be a mad rush this evening if Eloise didn't settle, she had packed her shoes and make-up bag and stopped at the dry cleaner's to collect her dress.

She had never been more excited to go on a date.

Ever.

Just as Elias had bought her coffee on many occasions, Beth bought one for Amanda.

It was gratefully received.

'Finn's been weaned off the ventilator,' Amanda said, and Beth beamed in delight. 'He's on CPAP and they're really pleased with him.'

It was fantastic news and they chatted away as they drank their coffee. Amanda said she would be more than happy to hang up Beth's dress in her room.

'I saw Elias in with her this morning, giving her a cuddle and telling her stories. He's such a great dad.'

'He really is.' Beth nodded.

That thought stayed with her as, having washed her hands, she headed through to NICU.

Eloise was fast asleep.

'She's had a busy morning,' Terri said, and brought Beth up to speed with all that had been discussed in the ward round. Terri was going through Eloise's care plan and little changes were happening. Soon she would have her first bath and it felt like a huge milestone.

She was still on the caffeine infusion but at a lower dose and she had put on more weight.

Every milestone felt like a huge achievement.

'Vince is really pleased with her. She's come a long way in four weeks.' Terri smiled. 'So how was your first night away from her?'

'I slept for ten hours straight,' Beth admitted guiltily. 'I thought I'd be awake, fretting, but I had a bath and I was out the minute my head hit the pillow.'

'Good for you. Don't get too used to it, though! You'll be on night feeds before you know it once she's home…'

And they were starting to speak of home.

Oh, it was still some time off, possibly four weeks, more likely five, but they were talking of it now and Beth knew that she needed to work out where home might be.

'Use this time to catch up on sleep and to get things sorted…'

Beth frowned, wondering if Terri knew just how fragile her relationship with Elias was, but as the nurse spoke on, she realised that wasn't what Terri had been referring to.

'Eloise wasn't due till March. It's still only January. If things had gone to plan you'd be tying up loose ends at work, buying baby stuff, getting your home ready for a baby. All that has been denied to you, so don't feel guilty about going home at night and getting some rest and doing all the things you'd have been doing had she not arrived so early.'

Beth nodded and looked down at Eloise— she was starting to wake up and was on the search for food. She had found her hand, which would keep her happy for a few moments.

'I'll go and make up her feed,' Beth said. Eloise now took a little food from a bottle but sucking exhausted her and she would fall asleep halfway through. What she couldn't manage would be fed to her down a small tube. But as Beth started to leave, Terri called her back. There was one other thing to discuss.

'Oh, can you let family and friends know that we can't provide updates on Eloise? We've had several phone calls to the unit over the last couple of days and Chloe has asked that you tell them to contact you for any news.'

'Sorry about that,' Beth said. 'My parents are allergic to mobile phones. My dad's coming in this afternoon, I'll remind him to tell Mum...'

'It's not just your parents,' Terri said.

'Then who?' Beth frowned as she tried to work out who it might be.

'Chloe didn't get a name, but there have been several phone calls. Maybe you can discuss it with Elias—perhaps his family are calling? I'm just saying that we take patient confidentiality very seriously here and at the risk of sounding rude we don't give out any information. We neither confirm nor deny that the patient is here, unless we are speaking directly to the next of kin.'

Perhaps Elias had told his parents, Beth thought as she gave Eloise her feed. The little girl had had a big day already. She'd been held by Elias, had had her IV reinserted and been examined on the ward round, so it was no great surprise that her feed didn't go well. Two gulps in, Eloise fell asleep and there was nothing Beth could do to wake her.

'I'll try,' Terri offered, but not even the experienced nurse could get Eloise to finish her feed and soon she was back in the incubator, being tube fed.

'What time is your father getting here?' Terri asked.

'One,' Beth said.

And she was tired of hiding.

Elias was a good dad, she wasn't going to deny his existence any more. Oh, she didn't want him here to meet her father but at the same time she wasn't going to pretend he was not around.

It was time to face things.

Elias was thinking the same thing.

He'd slept for a couple of hours but had woken and lain thinking about Beth's father visiting this afternoon. He wasn't in the least offended that Beth didn't want him there, given that he hadn't told his own parents yet, but he did want to meet her father at some point.

There was a buzz on the intercom and he ignored it. He had no idea what time it was and he rolled over to go back to sleep, but then he thought of Beth and wondered if she'd lost her key or if the doorman perhaps hadn't recognised her.

He picked up the internal phone by his bed and his voice was groggy.

'Yes.'

'There are two visitors here to see you, Dr Santini.'

'Who?'

He smothered a yawn but then sat upright when he was told who it was.

'Alvera and another woman. She chose not to give her name…'

Elias was out of bed and pulling on his jeans in an instant and a few moments later he opened the door to a tight-lipped Alvera and a woman he rarely saw unless she perceived him to be in trouble.

His mother.

'I think we need to talk,' Margarita said. 'Don't you?'

'You could have called to let me know you were coming,' Elias said, as the Queen and Alvera walked through to the lounge. Beth could have been here alone, he thought and, no, he didn't relish the thought of her dealing with his mother, particularly with the mood Margarita appeared to be in.

His absence had been a long one. Usually he

managed to get home every few months and that he had missed being home for his birthday had not gone down well, Andros had told him when he had called.

'There's a very good reason that I haven't been home,' Elias said, and as his mother took her place on the edge of the sofa with Alvera beside her, Elias took a seat in a chair. 'I recently became a father.'

Margarita didn't even blink so Elias pushed on.

'She was born ten weeks premature and it's been very harrowing for her mother. I've been trying to buy us some time before word gets out.'

Still his mother didn't reel in surprise; she just offered him the coldest stare. 'What on earth made you think you could handle this alone?'

'I've been handling it very well,' Elias said. He was proud of the fact that for almost four weeks he had managed to shield Beth and Eloise.

'So, for how long have you been seeing her mother?' Margarita asked.

'I don't need to run my dating history by you.'

'The press will want to know.'

Elias had thought of that. There was no denying that they would want details that were going to be rather awkward to provide.

'Tell me, Elias, how did you and this *lady* meet?'

He heard the sneer to her tone and he guessed that Beth would have been through similar when she'd told her father she was pregnant.

'I'm not going into all that now,' Elias said. 'Beth and I are working through things. I just need you to back off and let me sort it out.'

'You should have contacted me.' Alvera spoke now. 'As soon as she said that she was pregnant. There's a rumour going about that you delivered your own baby!'

Elias closed his eyes as he realised that they already knew. It was only ever going to be a matter of time before word got out.

'Just don't respond to the rumours,' Elias snapped. 'We've got a couple of weeks until we need to make it official.'

'You are not to register this birth without a DNA test,' Margarita hissed. 'You're not to sign anything until we have the results back.'

'I don't need a DNA test. I know that she's mine.'

'You might be happy to put your name to a one-night stand,' Margarita said, 'but I require more. I've told you to be careful, women will go to any lengths. Do you really think she just happened to be sitting on the beach that night?'

Elias frowned. He had never told them that the woman he had been photographed with on the beach was the mother of his child.

'How did you know it was Beth?'

Margarita didn't answer.

'How,' Elias asked, and there was a dark edge to his voice, 'did you know that?' He turned to Alvera. 'There will be no further conversation until you answer me.'

Alvera looked at the Queen, who gave her a nod, and Elias watched as she went in her case and took out some photos.

He'd been followed, and so too had Beth.

Only for a couple of days, it would seem, but long enough to find out that he was a regular visitor on NICU.

There were pictures of Beth shopping and of the two of them sitting by the lake, talking. Some were close-up images and he could see that both Beth and he were smiling. He could even remember what was being said at the time—they had been talking about their favourite meals and she had made him laugh.

Intensely personal moments had been captured.

There was even one of yesterday morning

when he had brought Beth from the hospital to his home.

'Just be glad it was our investigator that took these and not some journalist,' Margarita said.

Elias felt a smouldering anger build as he saw a photo of Beth getting out of the car, looking bewildered and rather concerned at the impressive address.

And then, as he flicked through the images, that anger roared as he saw there were still the photos of the night they had met.

'I said that these were to be destroyed,' Elias told Alvera, and he threw the images onto the coffee table. He'd tried to dismiss Beth's concerns about his power and wealth but they were, in fact, valid ones—the power of his family was intimidating and for a single mother trying to do the best by her infant it would be overwhelming.

For Elias it was the final straw and he stood up. 'You can leave now.'

He meant it but Margarita wasn't going anywhere.

'Elias, you have no choice but to listen. Our family has a reputation to uphold and there are certain things that need to be done, whether you like it or not. If this is your daughter it's going to be huge, but the most likely scenario is this woman is taking you—'

'Don't you dare insinuate that!' Elias furiously interrupted his mother. 'Beth doesn't even know that I'm royal. Not once have you asked how my daughter is doing. She's been in Intensive Care, with tubes and machines and holding on to life, and there were a couple of times we thought we might lose her.'

All the fears he had kept from Beth, everything he had kept in, he shouted out now.

'We have been through hell these past weeks and for you to worry about your reputation before asking after your granddaughter disgusts me.' He walked over to the fireplace and took down a photo of his own, the one Beth had had made for his birthday. 'There…' he said, and he watched his mother blink when she saw the tiny hand not even big enough to wrap around her father's finger. Then he went and got his phone and handed it to her. 'These are the photos you should have been demanding to see when you found out what was going on.'

He was white with fury but he watched as his mother looked through the photos and there was nothing in her expression that softened, no recognition that Eloise was related to her, and Elias understood her a little more.

It was all about duty.

Her duty had been to provide heirs, which she had. He thought of the nannies and the brief appearances by his parents. It was how they had been raised.

It is what it is.

Well, not any more.

'I shall take care of my family,' Elias told her. 'I don't need you to do that.'

'Actually, you do,' Margarita said. 'If you step down from duty there's going to be more interest than ever...'

'Can we take the emotion out of it?' Alvera suggested. 'Your Highness.' She looked at Elias. 'It's a simple cheek swab. You can speak with Beth, she can do the swab on the baby herself. We would have the results overnight. If they prove positive you will have the full support of the embassy and the palace to handle any press releases and to protect the mother and baby when the news gets out. The press will be camped outside your door otherwise.'

Elias knew this to be true.

'If you want privacy, this has to be done. I can take a swab from you now. You can go and speak with Beth, and explain it is the palace that demands this, not you.'

Her clinical, detached voice actually helped.

'I want to be the one to tell Beth,' Elias said. 'I'll tell her tonight and I'll do the swab on the condition you do everything to protect not just the baby but Beth. I want her reputation protected too. I mean it,' he warned.

His mother opened her mouth to protest but she must have seen the angry set of his features and heard his immutable tone.

'Very well,' Margareta conceded.

'Then let's get this done,' Alvera said and she pulled on some gloves and took out two swabs in plastic tubes. One he could give to Beth, Alvera explained. Elias opened his mouth so that she could take his sample with the other one.

And that was how Beth found him.

She'd wanted to speak with him about telling her father and also about the phone calls that Terri had mentioned.

Had he told his family? Beth had wondered as she'd walked the short distance to the apartment.

Was that who was calling?

There was something else niggling at her too.

The dream she'd had last night and the man walking on the pier.

She hadn't first seen Elias on the beach.

He had been walking from the yacht.

All this was whirring through her mind as

she stepped into the apartment, expecting to find Elias in bed asleep.

Beth might have no medical knowledge but she had watched enough crime shows and read enough books to know that she had walked in on Elias having a DNA swab.

It hurt.

So very much.

For all the problems they faced, that was one she'd thought they didn't have. She had been certain that Elias had accepted Eloise as his.

Everything seemed to be moving in slow motion. Elias stood as the woman replaced the swab in a tube and then he turned and saw her.

'Beth,' Elias said. 'Let's go through to the study and talk.'

'I don't want to talk to you!' Beth said in a voice that warned him not to attempt reason. She would work this out herself!

Beth took two steps forward and saw photos of herself and Elias on the coffee table and her eyes lit on the second swab. She swiped it and held it up.

'Were you going to do a quick cheek swab on her behind my back? Buy yourself some peace of mind and I'd never have had to know?'

'Beth, it's not what it looks like,' Elias said.

'It's *exactly* what it looks like.' She threw down the swab and then picked up a photo of she and Elias sitting by the lake and then threw it back down and glared at the older woman. 'What do you want?'

'I'm Elias's mother,' Margarita started to explain, but she didn't get very far!

'Well, it's *lovely* to meet you.' Beth's words were so loaded with sarcasm that Margarita's eyes widened—she certainly wasn't used to be spoken to like that. 'I shan't bother introducing myself when it would seem you already know plenty about me!'

Beth started to leave the room and he followed her.

'Don't walk off,' he told her.

'Don't try and stop me,' she countered. 'The one thing that I thought we had going for us,' Beth said, 'was that you knew Eloise was yours.'

'I requested it,' Margarita said.

'You need a test to pacify your mother?' Beth walked over to the coffee table and picked up the sterile swab and put it in her bag. 'You'll get your sample,' Beth said.

'I'll come with you.' Elias went for his coat.

'I can make my own way, thank you,' Beth said, and stalked off.

'Sort it, Elias,' his mother commanded.

'Oh, I intend to.' Elias nodded.

But he'd do it his way.

CHAPTER FIFTEEN

WHEN YOU HAD a baby on the NICU ward there weren't an awful lot of places that you could run off to, to hide and lick your wounds.

In addition, her father would arrive soon and so Beth made her way back to St Patrick's, where she sat by Eloise's incubator and stared at her daughter, trying to make sense of what had just taken place.

She had been ready to tell her father about Elias, she had actually started to believe in their relationship.

Not now.

She had been sure that he fully accepted that Eloise was his, but as she thought about it she could see that he had stalled on getting her birth registered.

Could she blame him for doubting that Eloise was his? They had been a one-night stand after all.

And, whether or not he believed her, he had

stood by her through these difficult weeks. He had been there night and day for both Eloise and herself.

She looked at her phone and, no, he hadn't called, and nor had he made any attempt to stop her from leaving.

Well, if they needed proof they could have it.

She took out the swab and read the instructions and it was supposed to be taken before food or drink.

'Are you okay, Beth?' Terri asked.

Terri had been the most wonderful support this past month. She had seen Beth at her lowest and had been a constant strength and Beth trusted her with her daughter's life, so she could trust her with this.

'Elias wants me to take a DNA swab from Eloise, or rather his mother does.'

Yes, Terri had seen it all working here and she gave Beth a gentle smile.

'Sometimes people need that extra assurance,' Terri said.

'Can you do it for me?' Beth asked.

'I can't.' Terri shook her head. 'Unless it's ordered. But I can be with you while you do it.'

It felt like an insult to her daughter as she took it. 'Sorry,' Beth said to Eloise, and then, job done, she had a little cry as she put the tube in her bag.

'Beth?' She jumped as Chloe came over and she quickly wiped her eyes. 'Your father's here.'

It had to be today that he came!

She hadn't seen her father since the terrible argument the day she'd gone to Edinburgh and now she went to the small waiting room at the front of the unit.

He was wearing a long grey coat and carrying a black holdall.

'Beth.' He nodded.

At least he wasn't calling her Elizabeth now but he still couldn't look her in the eye.

'Hi, Dad.'

'I've got a few things for you.' He held up the bag. 'And for a woman named Amanda?'

Indeed, he did have a few things. Beth took him through to the parents' lounge and the fridge was soon full of containers of food from home.

'Amanda will be thrilled,' Beth said. 'She's been here for so long and is tired of living off takeaways.'

'Well, there's plenty for the both of you,' Donald said. 'Is this where you're staying? Why don't you show me around?'

And it wasn't because she'd recently moved

in with Elias that she declined her father's request, rather it was because she realised he was nervous about meeting Eloise.

'Come on, Dad,' Beth said. 'Let's go and see her.'

Donald washed his hands over and over and then they made their way into NICU. Beth took her stoic father's arm as he fell apart.

'Well, that was always going to happen,' Donald said, and tears filled his eyes. 'I knew I'd melt the moment I saw her. She's so small.'

'She's a lot bigger than she was,' Beth said.

'And she looks a lot like you did. Everyone's asking after her,' he said. 'And after you.'

'Well, you can tell them that we're both doing fine.'

'Has she been registered?'

'Not yet.'

'Beth!' Her father was shocked. He was prompt about filling out forms and a stickler for things such as this. 'It needs to be done. I can come with you now.'

'No, we're going to wait.'

'We?'

And no matter how hurt she was, Elias was a good father.

And she would no longer hide things.

'Her father has been here every day,' Beth told him.

'You remembered his surname, then,' Donald said with a tart edge.

'No, he worked out mine.' She wanted to tell her father that Elias had even come to the church to try and find her, that he had delivered their baby, but she just didn't know where to start. 'He's been there every step of the way for Eloise and me...'

'I was sick. I would have been here sooner,' Donald said, and she watched as her father looked down at his granddaughter and the tears rolled down his cheeks.

'That wasn't a dig at you, Dad. I know you've been unwell. Elias said that you were right to stay away. He's a doctor, he knows things that I don't. All I'm saying is that, since Eloise has been born, he's been there and we're trying to sort things out, to work things out.'

'Is that why you haven't registered the birth?' Her father was a shrewd man. 'Does he not want to put his name to his mistake?'

'Please, Dad, don't call her a mistake.'

'I didn't mean that. I'm just so angry at him. Is he questioning that she's his?'

Beth didn't answer, she didn't want to throw fuel on the fire, but her silence said it all and Donald saw that Beth's eyes were shiny with new tears so he did not press her further.

Donald was incensed, though.

He stayed till after five and though Beth was glad that he had visited and was taken with Eloise, it was all rather tense. It was a relief when it was time for him to go.

'You know I like to get to the train station in plenty of time,' Donald said as he put on his coat.

'I know that you do.'

Beth walked him to the exit of the NICU.

'I'll come with your mother next week.'

'I'd like that.'

'Your daughter's very beautiful,' he told her, but then, instead of walking off, he took a deep breath. 'Come home to the manse, Beth. Once Eloise is ready to leave the hospital, you're to come home. We'll take care of you both.'

These were the words she'd wanted to hear all those months ago, but now they weren't needed. Beth knew she could take care of her daughter, with or without Elias's support.

She wanted it to be with him, though.

Even hurt and confused by his actions today, Beth knew that she loved him.

She had from the start.

Beth had never believed in love at first sight but she did now.

It wasn't Elias's fault he didn't feel the same but she hoped, for them, that love and trust could somehow grow.

'Her father and I have a lot to work out,' Beth said, and she told Donald the truth. 'He's a good man, Dad.'

'He's *no* man,' Donald said.

The subject was closed.

But Elias was indeed a man.

As Donald walked out of the NICU unit he startled slightly when he saw a rather tall, somewhat familiar, dark-haired man walking towards him.

He'd seen him before, sitting in his congregation.

A man with his dark Mediterranean good looks tended to stand out in a small Scottish church.

'Reverend Foster,' Elias introduced himself. 'I'm Elias Santini.' He was about to offer his hand but knew from the glare of frosty blue eyes it would not be accepted. 'I'd like to apologise for the stress and embarrassment that I've caused to your family.'

'And continue to do so,' Donald said. 'Why has her birth not been registered? How dare you question that Eloise is yours.'

Oh, this was going to be hard.

'I've never questioned that she's mine,' Elias calmly told him. 'But my family are displeased. Can we go somewhere to speak?'

Donald would not be making his train.

They sat in the hospital canteen and Elias offered to get them a coffee.

'I'm here to talk,' Donald said, and seemed to be declining Elias's offer. But then those hours on NICU *had* been warm and draining… 'I'll have a cup of tea.'

Elias had the same and talk they did.

He told Donald about his parents and also his title, and he admitted that Beth still didn't know.

'Your title doesn't impress me,' Donald warned.

'I know it doesn't,' Elias said, 'and I know that it won't impress Beth either. She's going to be upset at first when she finds out and I can understand why.'

'It is what it is,' Donald said, as he so often did when things went wrong for a member of his flock and it was time to start the repair work.

'You came to my church, didn't you?'

Elias nodded.

'Well, did you listen to what I said?' the reverend asked, for he had changed his sermon at the last moment, and had turned to Corinthians, just in case the gentleman sitting at the back was who he thought it might be.

'I did.' Elias thought about it for a moment.

'And now I'm a father to a daughter I have to say I tend to agree.'

He couldn't say the reverend smiled but there was a small nod and Elias pushed on.

He told him about the two roles he had juggled as a royal prince and also as a doctor. He told him about the two worlds he lived in and that he hoped Reverend Foster would give his permission for his daughter to join him.

Elias did the right thing, albeit several months too late, but Donald admired that he had. And so, in the end and after thought, Donald acquiesced. 'You'll take good care of my daughter?'

Elias nodded. 'I will.'

'Better care,' Donald said, and pointed his finger in warning.

Oh, he would.

And they spoke for a little while about practicalities and it was all rather uncomfortable but all very polite.

'I'd appreciate it if you didn't tell Beth that we've spoken just yet.'

Donald considered that for a moment and then gave a nod. 'I need to go. I've already missed one train. If I'm going to make it for the next one, I need to get on.'

'I can give you a lift—' Elias started, but was interrupted.

'I'll make my own way, thank you.'

Beth was certainly her father's daughter, Elias thought, and smiled as the reverend stalked off.

There was no DNA test needed there either!

And if he'd thought Reverend Foster hard work, Elias knew he still had a certain angry redhead to face.

First, though, he went home and changed into a suit for their night out.

He walked into the NICU, saw her shoulders stiffen as he approached and she turned her back on him.

It was time to fight fire with fire.

'Aren't you ready?'

'For what?'

'We're going out, remember.'

'I don't think so.'

'Well, I do,' Elias said. 'You really don't like confrontation, do you, Beth? I accept you've needed to focus on Eloise these past weeks but it's time now to talk about us.'

He was so bloody confident. There was Eloise kicking her little legs and he squirted his hands with some alcohol rub and put them into the incubator and he said good evening to his daughter, who was wide awake and sucking on her hand.

He glanced up at Beth, who still stood there.

She was holding a bottle for Eloise and had clearly been about to get her out for a feed.

'We're going out for dinner.'

'No, Elias, we're not.' She took the swab out of her bag and put it on top of the incubator. 'There's your swab. I'm not hungry all of a sudden. Anyway, Eloise needs to be fed.'

'I can do that while you get changed.'

He took both the bottle and the excuse from Beth and then sat himself in the large chair that was brought over for such occasions.

Terri took little Eloise out of her incubator and handed her to Elias. 'You might get milk on your suit.'

'That's fine.'

And he looked at Beth, who was as obstinate and as indignant as her father and refusing to jump to his command.

He still hadn't quite worked out how to tell her but, audience or no audience, as he fed Eloise her bottle, he knew he had to now.

He looked down at his daughter.

'Once upon a time...' he told her, as he so often did, but then the story changed and he told Eloise the truth. 'There was a prince...a very unhappy prince...'

CHAPTER SIXTEEN

BETH WAS BUSYING herself making up the cot as he told Eloise her bedtime story.

'Well, the Prince had been told he had to give up the job he loved and return to his country. Once there, he partied far too hard and got into trouble. A lot of it. His parents wanted him to settle down and marry and he was supposed to be photographed dancing with a princess, but the Prince had had enough and walked off the royal yacht and was photographed dancing with the wrong woman...'

And Beth, who was putting the little pink bear with the tiara back in its regular spot, stilled.

Her face was as white as the night she'd been rushed into Accident and Emergency.

Somewhere in her mind Beth conceded she had already known. He *had* come from the yacht that night. And she'd known from speaking with Mr Costas that there were royals on that yacht. She had simply not been ready to face things and she didn't feel ready to now.

She wanted to grab her baby and run, yet she just stood there as Elias snuggled Eloise into his arms.

'It's going to be okay,' he told her.

And all she could think of was that there were photos of them together that night and that nothing could ever be normal for her baby.

'Beth,' Elias said, and his voice was very even and calm. 'Go and get ready, we're going out.'

And they had to go out, Beth knew.

It was time to face things.

On legs that were shaking Beth made it out to the parents' room, where Amanda was tucking into homemade soup and potato scones.

'Have you come for the dress?'

Beth nodded and tried to carry on as normal but it was very hard to make small talk with Amanda. Soon, though, she had made it into Amanda's room and sat on the edge of the bed for a moment, trying to collect herself.

All she wanted, all she had *ever* wanted for Eloise was a normal, healthy life.

She'd nearly managed the latter but it would seem the former was something she was never going to be able to provide.

Somehow Beth dressed and put on some

make-up. She added her dangly earrings and then she looked in the mirror.

The last time she had worn this dress she'd been pregnant with no idea what was to come that night.

She was more nervous now than she had been then as she headed back out for her first date with her baby's father. She'd once been so looking forward to it, so excited by the prospect of a date. Now she was dreading it.

And yet as she walked through the unit there was Elias, putting Eloise back in her incubator and looking so handsome in his suit and so unfazed. And there was her beautiful baby, fast asleep and content with the world.

Beth looked at the little princess teddy in the incubator and she understood why he had chosen it.

He'd been carrying this burden for weeks.

And, yes, it felt like a burden.

'Have a great night,' Terri told them. 'Any problems, you'll be contacted but I don't expect there to be. And, remember, Eloise is in very good hands.'

She was.

Terri knew about Elias.

Of course she knew.

Elias Santini had delivered his own baby— she knew that as fact. And, just this very morning, her heart had sunk as she'd read a small news article.

Yes, Terri had seen a lot of things in her time on the NICU.

She just hoped very much that this young couple could make it through.

It was a cold night. They walked the short distance to the restaurant he had chosen and Beth was silent for a while.

'What does this mean for Eloise?' she finally asked. 'Does that make her a princess?'

'She's our daughter first,' Elias said. 'But yes.'

'I don't want her photographed,' Beth said, and then she stopped walking as the enormity of it all started to take hold. 'Those pictures of the night we met...'

'I've told them that they're to be destroyed.'

'That doesn't mean a thing,' Beth said in a choked voice. 'They'll surface later.' She had read about such things. She felt sick at the thought of her father and the Elders seeing what had taken place that night.

'Beth, they weren't terrible photos...'

'Perhaps not for you,' Beth angrily countered. 'I can't do this.'

'Why?'

'We had a one-night stand. When they find out that—?'

'That's why I agreed to the DNA. It wasn't to pacify my mother, it was to get them on side so that I could take better care of you both. The palace can sort it...'

'They can't gloss over this,' she said. 'We've been apart for months.' She could just picture it now. It had been bad enough when her father had found out but to have it played out in the papers... She thought of the Elders and the parishioners reading salacious versions of her one-night stand, with photos attached. It was too much and she told him so.

'We can work through it,' Elias said. 'For now, let's just have a nice night.'

And Beth rolled her eyes.

It was ruined already.

As they stepped into the restaurant, there was a pianist but the music was unobtrusive and she was helped out of her coat.

They were led to a very private table at the back and waiting for them was an icy bucket of champagne, but Beth shook her head. 'I don't want any.'

'Oh, yes, you do,' he said. 'Beth, this is a date and the last one we had we kicked things off with champagne...'

'That wasn't a date,' she said. 'That was sex.'

'Good, wasn't it?'

And when he smiled like that, when he made her recall it like that, it made her want to smile too, but she covered it by taking a sip of her drink.

It tasted delicious and icy—it had been a very long time since she'd drunk champagne.

Since Eloise's conception, in fact.

'You'd come from the yacht the night we met?'

Elias nodded. 'I was supposed to be seen with Sophie that night. We were going to set the ball rolling and neither of us wanted that. She never said so, of course, but I could tell and I knew I didn't want to settle down.'

So much had changed since then.

Beth looked through the menu and she groaned when she saw that they had Chicken Provençal. It was her favourite food ever, if done right.

'We had this French couple come to stay at the manse,' Beth told him. 'My mum thinks she can make it but she can't.' Beth smiled. 'The village shop does their version of *herbes de Provence* but it doesn't have lavender in it and she uses white wine vinegar…'

'You told me.'

'So I did.' Beth smiled.

For all they didn't know about each other, they had chatted a lot on their walks.

Their meals were served and Beth took a taste of hers. Oh, this one had lavender! It was delectable and as she ate her meal he told her how leaving medicine had hurt.

'I was younger then and the palace didn't support me, they just wanted me back in Medrindos. I was there for two years, living this idle, pointless life…'

And she thought how he'd said that medicine was worthwhile.

'After I met you I told them I was returning to London. I go home for formal occasions and I love it, but they don't need me there full-time. My father is a strong leader, he'll be around for years. Then there's my older brother… I don't want to be an idle royal. I've applied to work full-time in London…' He saw her fork pause midway to her mouth. 'I can apply in Edinburgh if you prefer…'

'You'd move to Edinburgh?'

'If that's what you want.' Elias nodded. 'Beth, I'm going to do all I can to make sure that you and Eloise get the privacy you deserve and I want her to have a happy life just as much as you.'

Beth recalled how austere his so-called privileged upbringing had been and she thought of his mother sitting there on the sofa, so immutable and cold.

'I was rude to your mother.'

'It gave me a smile.'

'I don't know how my family will take the news. My father—'

'Will be fine.'

Beth gave a hollow laugh.

'He *was* fine, in fact. Well, a bit shocked at first and he told me that my title doesn't impress him one iota…'

'You've spoken with him?'

'Yes.' He nodded. 'We had tea! And I refrained from telling him that *his* title terrifies me!'

Beth laughed but it changed.

He had spoken with her father. She had wanted to be there, to somehow control the conversation and hold everybody back…

'What did he say?'

'That I'm to take better care of you in the future,' Elias said. 'And I intend to. Beth, I just wanted to have a few weeks together while we could just be us.'

She thought of the burden he had carried to give them some privacy and space.

Yes, perhaps he should have told her sooner but she tried to picture dealing with this conversation even a week ago.

She couldn't have.

He had shielded them from so much.

Beth was ready to deal with it now.

'I think I knew,' Beth admitted. 'Not all of it but I knew there was more to come.' She was honest then. 'I wanted to fall in love with *you* first.'

And it was the nicest thing anyone had ever said to him and he took her hand.

'It's gorgeous here,' Beth admitted, and she looked around at her surroundings. 'It's perfect.'

It was good to be out.

In fact, it felt like a date.

The best date she had ever had.

Only it was a very odd first date indeed because he let go of her hand, went into his pocket and took out a ring.

Not one his mother would have chosen, for that would have meant it came from Medrindos and was not truly hers.

This came from him.

It was the dark ruby of her earrings and the same rose gold that she loved; it was subtle and beautiful and a little old-fashioned. She stared at it but with all the revelations of today the moment was spoiled.

'I don't want you to marry me just because

it's the right thing to do,' she said. 'I don't want to be married just to avoid a scandal or—'

'Beth,' he broke in. 'Soon you will find out my reputation and, believe me, you'll know that I don't do the right thing. I am arrogant and stubborn, and, if I didn't want to be married, you would receive a monthly account from the palace and it would all be discreetly dealt with. I come from a very long line of royalty with mistresses and bastards...'

'Really?'

'Alvera is used to the trouble my family creates. That's why she wanted the DNA to be done. I was opposed to it but I also knew that if we do work out, and I believe we shall, then it's going to be big news...'

She felt nerves leap in her stomach.

Nice nerves, though.

'You asked my dad if you could marry me?'

When Rory had hinted that he might be going to speak with her father, panic had hit.

That Elias already had, that he had done all he could to sort things out, meant the world to her.

'I love you.' Elias said the words he had never said before. The thought of being tied down to one person for the rest of his life had been overwhelming. It wasn't now. 'And I'm going to do everything I can to shield you and

Eloise. I love my country and I want to do the right thing by them, but know that you two will always come first. Marry me, Beth, but only if you really want to.'

'I do.'

More than anything.

'Don't be scared.'

And she looked up from the ring to him and saw in his eyes the concern that had been there the night she had given birth. It was more than concern, it was love.

'Come on.' Elias stood and held out his hand. 'Let's dance.'

They did.

It was the best first date in the world.

He held her on the dance floor, twirled her and she felt his hand on her back to signal a dip. She let herself fall and then he pulled her close in.

Beth stared at the man she had possibly loved on sight. They knew each other now.

Not everything, of course, but the parts that mattered and the rest they would take their time to find out.

And even without fully knowing him, from the look in his eyes she knew she was about to be kissed and she wanted that very much. She could feel the heat of his palms on her waist.

They were in that delicious space where they felt as if they were the only two in the room.

Except they weren't and, Elias knew, he would take the very best care of her.

Of them.

His little family.

'Come on,' he said, and they walked back to the table. He called for the bill, which he signed, and then Beth was helped into her coat.

They stepped out of the restaurant and he called the hospital to be told that Eloise was sleeping peacefully. But instead of taking her hand and taking her home, he walked her to a luxurious hotel.

'All your things are there...' He handed her the key to her suite.

'I don't understand,' Beth said.

'I told your father that I'd do this right, and that means, as much as I want you in my bed tonight, that it's better that you don't live with me just yet.'

She wanted to be in his bed so much and yet there was a flurry of relief for Beth because if this was going to get out at some point, she wanted her father to be proud not just of her but of them.

There was no doubting their desire, and that he was prepared to wait was a compliment this time. He knew she was tired, and that Eloise wasn't out of the woods just yet.

It hadn't been even a month since their lives had changed for ever.

'Concentrate on Eloise,' Elias said, 'and focus on yourself. We can have our walks and go out at night and I'll take care of the wedding.'

'You're going to take care of the wedding?'

'Yes. You've got enough to deal with.'

She had.

Elias really had thought of everything.

He saw her to her door and there she faced him, hardly able to believe just how wonderful the night had been.

'It's been perfect,' she said. 'From the food, to the dancing.' And then she looked down at her ring. 'Right down to this. I love rose gold.'

'I know that you do. Aren't you glad that I didn't take you skiing to propose?'

And then she frowned. 'Elias?'

He smiled as for Beth the penny dropped.

'*You're* my lazy client?'

'I am.'

'You emailed me to arrange the perfect proposal?'

'I did.'

But that had been before she'd had Eloise.

'Why?'

'Because I've been wanting to propose for a very long time. It was great to get back to medicine but as much as I was enjoying it, I just couldn't get you out of my head. I made the decision to go up to Dunroath and see if you felt the same. The reason I didn't speak to your father after the service was because I decided to find you myself. I found your website. I loved you then, Beth. I realised that I've loved you since the moment we met.'

And she had loved him just the same.

He kissed her at her door and she finally went in and Beth was crying happy tears as she realised the truth.

He hadn't just been looking for her these past months, he'd found her.

Through all those lonely times Elias had been working his way back to her side.

CHAPTER SEVENTEEN

Royal Prince Elias Santini Delivers His Own Baby!

The palace has confirmed that Prince Elias of Medrindos, who is second in line to the throne, did indeed deliver his own baby nearly six weeks ago.

His fiancée, Elizabeth Foster, went into premature labour early in January and gave birth to a daughter.

The palace states that the engagement and birth were not initially announced in order to ensure the young family's privacy during this tumultuous time.

The palace is happy to confirm that Princess Eloise of Medrindos is now doing well but request that her privacy is maintained.

BETH SAT IN the postnatal clinic and read the article on her phone and smiled.

All the hurt, all the doubts, even a hint at a mistake had been removed and glossed over.

And that was how she felt—deliciously glossed.

Somehow they had found each other here in the NICU.

Elias had been right not to tell her at first, she now realised.

They had shut the world out and focussed on their baby and also on finding each other, knowing each other.

'Elizabeth Foster!'

She looked up as her name was called and went through for her postnatal check-up.

The doctor was lovely and looked through her notes.

'You had quite a time of it, didn't you?'

'I did.' Beth nodded. 'She's doing very well now. Well, she had a bit of a setback last week but she's turned the corner.'

Eloise had developed a chest infection and for two nights Beth had moved back to the parents' wing. It hadn't all been plain sailing but she and Elias had got through it. Now there was talk of Eloise going home in the next couple of weeks.

'How are you doing?'

'I'm doing well.' Beth nodded.

She had her check-up and the doctor answered her questions. No, there were no guarantees that it might not happen again with the next baby, but any subsequent pregnancies would be monitored closely.

And that was that.

Apart from one thing.

'Have you registered the birth?' the doctor checked.

'We're doing that tomorrow,' Beth said.

'Well, make sure you do. You've only got a couple of days left.'

'I shall.'

'So, are you headed back up to the NICU?' the doctor asked as she closed up her file.

'Actually, no.' Beth shook her head and smiled. 'I'm getting married in an hour's time!'

There would be another announcement for the palace to make very soon, but by then it would all be done.

She had always thought she would marry in the small church at home. And when Elias had asked her to marry him, terror had gripped her that a formal royal wedding would be expected.

These were exceptional circumstances, though, and so mountains had been moved.

And now, two weeks before Eloise was hopefully to be discharged home, there was another, rather special event taking place.

It was to be the tiniest of weddings.

Though she would have loved to have had more time to prepare, it was important to both of them as well as to their families that they marry. Eloise needed to officially have her father's name and they would be husband and wife.

Even though she was an events planner, there hadn't been time to organise this and she had left it to Elias. Jean had pinned and taken in the family wedding dress. Beth had this morning, before her Outpatients appointment, been to have her hair put up. Her mother had brought a posy of snowdrops from the gardens of the manse.

When Elias had told her the date he had arranged, Beth's heart had soared because she was a romantic at heart, but he had blinked in surprise when she had said it was Valentine's Day.

'Well, maybe we can go out for dinner afterwards,' Elias had said. 'But we'll have my family here and yours,' he'd pointed out.

Yes, this was a wedding to make it official, nothing more. Even so, as she stood on her father's arm at the door of the hospital chapel she was excited to be marrying the man of her dreams.

She was wearing a very simple dress in cream, with a small scoop neck and a thin length of tartan tied beneath her bust. She also had on the earrings she had worn on the night that she and Elias had met.

'You look lovely,' her father said, and, which was terribly important to Beth, he could now look her in the eye. 'Are you ready?'

'I am.'

'You're not nervous?' he checked, and Beth shook her head.

They would be in and out in five minutes. It was a formality, that was all.

It was *so* much more than that, she found out as she walked in.

There were only a few pews but at the end of each one was a small posy of gardenias tied with the same tartan as her dress, and the scent of them filled the tiny chapel.

The pews were filled, not just with staff and friends they had made over the weeks in NICU, as Beth had expected, but with friends from her childhood and Voula and George Costas were there too.

It was almost like being home.

And there were Elias's parents and family,

all here to celebrate this special day and, best of all, there was Elias.

He had done all he could to give her the wedding of her dreams.

It was better than her dreams, for she was marrying him.

He was dressed proudly in a formal military uniform, as he had served and would serve his country.

As she walked towards him she made a very demure bride and he loved this private, modest woman who came alive to his touch.

To Beth he looked more handsome than ever in his uniform and boots, and she blushed as she joined him. There was a small lull in proceedings as Donald moved from being father of the bride to the front of the chapel.

There were two officiators. There was Beth's father and there was a priest from Medrindos. Though low key, this wedding was very official.

'You look wonderful,' Elias said, as the reverend took his place.

'So do you.' Beth smiled. 'How on earth did you get gardenias in February?'

'Did I forget to tell you that there are some perks to being royal?'

And to think she had thought it would be a hastily arranged wedding.

'You knew it was Valentine's Day when you booked it?'

'Of course I did,' he said. 'It works out well—I'll never forget our anniversary.'

He made her smile and he made her happy and that he'd paid such loving attention during those conversations at the pond meant so much to Beth.

She thought of her lazy client who had actually been him all along, and of course he would ensure her wedding was perfect!

And then the service started and just when she thought it was time to be serious Beth got another surprise.

'Who giveth this woman to marry this man?' Donald asked, and then looked up at the congregation. 'Oh, that would be me.'

And she had never, on that awful black day when she had left home in disgrace, thought she might hear one of her father's terrible jokes and be giggling at it again.

But, then, that was what a certain little lady had done.

Eloise was slowly working her magic on them all.

Her father had decided a week was too long between visits and now they came to London on Monday and Friday. Elias had been right to move Beth to a suite in the hotel, it made things so much easier with her family. In addition, the press were hovering.

But together they were working it out.

Even Margarita was proving a more loving grandparent than she had been a parent. She had not only given Eloise a bottle but also had been seen singing to her.

But today was about them, for life changed today.

Then again it had changed so many times since she had met Elias.

And even if some of the changes had felt like agony at the time, each change had been for the better.

From being left alone that morning after their one-night stand to finding out now that she was very much loved.

Beth looked at Elias as she recited her vows and the last one was special indeed. 'And all my worldly goods with thee I share.'

Her love and Eloise were all she really had but they were the most treasured gifts he had ever received.

And then Donald announced that they were husband and wife.

'You may kiss your bride,' Donald said.

And if Beth made a very demure bride, Elias was a surprisingly reticent groom.

All present were aware he had *more* than

kissed the bride in the past and so today he gave her a soft, loving kiss that confirmed their vows.

'My father approves,' Beth said out of the corner of her mouth as they walked back down the aisle.

'Wait till I get you home.'

'We're going out with our parents,' she reminded him, but Elias just smiled.

There was a small reception for guests to congratulate the happy pair and an opportunity for photos too.

'I've invited Margarita and Bruno to come and spend some time at the manse,' Donald said.

'They're coming back tonight.' Jean nodded.

The manse was always ready for guests and Beth smiled at the thought of two very different families making the effort to get to know each other. It was to be the perfect Valentine's Day wedding and honeymoon night after all.

Still, there was one person they both ached to see and very soon they were up on NICU.

Beth put her posy of snowdrops in a vase in the parents' room and then, having washed their hands, they walked through the unit to see their baby. As they did so, Beth thought of how far Eloise had come.

Past the dark room filled with spare cots they walked and then past the critical care infants, to a room that meant their daughter was a little closer to being allowed home.

'She's asleep.' The nurse smiled when she saw the happy couple.

So she was.

And she was utterly delightful.

There were changes every day and now her little cheeks were filling out.

Eloise was starting to do all the things a full-term baby did.

'Mummy and Daddy love you,' Elias said, the same words he had used on that terrifying first night. Though the feelings were the same, the words came more naturally now and were said without so much fear. 'You'll be home soon.'

But now it was time for them.

He did everything right.

Elias carried her through the door but did not put her down, taking her straight through to the bedroom.

They hadn't waited until marriage, they had simply waited till the time was right.

And it was now.

Eloise was safe and doing well, there were flowers and champagne but Beth would notice them later; instead, she trembled as he turned her round. She stood there, feeling dizzy with anticipation as she heard him undress.

One long leather boot thudded to the floor and then the other, and when she knew he was naked she did not turn round; instead, she waited as he undid every tiny button that ran the length of her spine till the dress dropped to the floor.

She stood shaking as he peeled off her underwear and then finally he turned her to him and his eyes blazed with desire.

'I've missed you,' he told her.

'And I've missed you,' Beth said.

'But you're home now,' he said, and properly kissed his bride.

First Elias kissed her mouth, her face and her eyes as he removed the grips in her hair till it tumbled down her shoulders.

His hands roamed her body and hers reacquainted themselves with his. She felt the solid chest she had wept on and the strong arms that had wrapped around her during such difficult times.

Every touch he delivered made her shiver, every caress made her knees want to fold and her body become weak. He kissed her hard till she was on the bed and then as she lay there he kissed her body till she writhed in longing.

He kissed her calves, the insides of her knees and she started to moan as he kissed her inner thighs. And Beth had never been kissed *there* before.

'Just enjoy,' Elias murmured to her, realising how little she'd been loved.

They had a lifetime to catch up.

She was tense and resisting till his tongue swirled her into heaven, but then, as she moaned, he withdrew the pleasure and he leant over her. There was no question if it was too soon or if she was ready, she needed him inside her.

Side on, they faced each other, and he moved her leg so that it was over his thigh. He watched for pain as he slowly took her.

There was no pain, just a building desire that only he could ever satisfy.

And he did.

'I love you,' he said, and she knew that he did.

He loved every side of her that she could only reveal to him.

'I want you so much,' she told him.

She always had, from the moment they had met, and there was no need to fight it now.

Elias took her right to the edge, and then they shattered together, high on sensation.

They were husband and wife together for ever and, most importantly, they knew this was love.

EPILOGUE

THE MOST SENSIBLE thing Beth had done, even if it had hurt at the time, had been to swab her daughter's cheek.

The palace authorities had moved into action and it felt as though a cloak of protection had been placed around them.

Eloise had been discharged from the hospital without fanfare and they had commenced family life.

Elias worked at The Royal, and had been teased a little by some of the staff there when they'd found out, but they all supported and protected him. Beth had managed to plan and execute Gemma's stunning June wedding and then Beth, Elias and Eloise had headed off for a gorgeous week in Dunroath, staying at the manse.

Now they were, for the first time, at the palace.

Eloise was eight months old and today Queen Margarita turned sixty.

There were to be several formal celebrations and it had been decided that after an official luncheon Beth and Eloise would stand with the family on the balcony.

This way Eloise wouldn't be the centre of attention.

'She's a bit grumpy,' Beth said. 'I doubt she'll smile.'

'Well, she just got her first tooth,' Elias pointed out. 'She's not a circus act, it doesn't matter if she's cross.'

He could remember standing there, forcing a smile, and he would not insist on the same for Eloise. She'd had a sleep after lunch and they'd done their best to make sure she was happy and relaxed, but there was no way of knowing how she'd respond to the cheers of the crowd.

'She looks gorgeous,' Elias said. 'And so do you.'

Beth was wearing a very simple dress in willow green. She'd chosen a wraparound one but had been advised it might not be the best choice if Eloise grabbed the neckline.

'You don't want to flash to the people.' Elias had grinned.

No.

So now she stood, holding Eloise, as the French doors that led to the balcony opened and Margarita and Bruno stepped out to cheers that increased as the rest of the family joined them.

'You're doing fine,' Elias said, and she felt his warm palm in the small of her back.

He had always been told that he led a privileged life but now, as he stood on the balcony with his family beside him, he *felt* privileged indeed.

They were both amazing.

Beth held on to Eloise, who wasn't bothered in the least by the noise from the crowd—she'd spent weeks attached to very loud alarms after all.

No, Eloise was far more interested in Yaya's lovely crown. It was sparkly and pretty and so too today was Yaya.

Eloise knew she was the apple of Margarita's eye and she decided she wanted a cuddle. *Now, please!*

She held out her arms and the Queen stared ahead, so Eloise held them out some more.

And who could resist?

The crowd cheered louder as they saw a different side to their Queen as she took Eloise in her arms and helped her to wave.

It was a precious moment indeed and Beth forgot her nerves and laughed.

Yes, she could do this!

They were still laughing about it as they tucked Eloise in for a nap and she reached for her little pink bear.

'She's amazing,' Elias said. 'I don't think anyone ever thought they'd see my mother laugh like that.'

'It was fun.' Beth smiled and they closed the door on their sleeping child.

'I've got a surprise for you,' Elias told her.

Life with Elias was one big, delicious surprise, Beth thought as they stepped into their bedroom.

It was magnificent.

The palace was set high on a cliff and they had an entire wing just for them to be a family whenever they were home.

The shutters were open but it wasn't the glittering Mediterranean that caught her eye there, no, it was something else.

Beth had been right, photos did surface again, and there it was, blown up and huge on their palace bedroom wall.

A photo of Elias and Beth dancing in the ocean on the night they had met.

It was black and white, but only because it was night.

As she stared she could see the red tint of her hair as it trailed in the water, and his hand beneath her spine.

Beth was so glad now that that moment had been captured—the first time she had let herself fall.

And as he pulled her in for a kiss she was still falling for him.

Every day, every night they fell deeper and deeper in love.

* * * * *

If you enjoyed
THEIR SECRET ROYAL BABY,
don't miss Carol Marinelli's spectacular
100th book

THE INNOCENT'S SECRET BABY

Available now!

If you enjoyed this story,
check out these other great reads from
Carol Marinelli

PLAYBOY ON HER CHRISTMAS LIST
SEDUCED BY THE SHEIKH SURGEON
THE SHEIKH'S BABY SCANDAL
DI SIONE'S INNOCENT CONQUEST

All available now!